Now *I* was the alien....

I'll never forget my first day at school here. My father led me in and stood me next to Darva Preet, the teacher. She smiled that strange Kwarkissian smile, reached down one of her six arms to take my hand, then turned to the room and cried: "Class! Class! Come to order! I want you to meet our new student— the alien you've all heard so much about!"

I began to blush. It was still hard to think of myself as an alien. But of course, that's what I was: The only kid from Earth on a planet full of people that *I* had considered aliens until I got here. Now that I was on Kwarkis, the situation was reversed. Now *I* was the alien.

Other Bruce Coville anthologies from Scholastic include:

Bruce Coville's Book of Monsters

and coming soon:

Bruce Coville's Book of Ghosts
Bruce Coville's Book of Nightmares

BRUCE COVILLE'S BOOK OF

ALIENS
TALES TO WARP YOUR MIND

Compiled and edited by
Bruce Coville

Illustrated by
John Pierard

A GLC Book

AN
APPLE
PAPERBACK

SCHOLASTIC INC.
New York Toronto London Auckland Sydney

For Lisa, who suffers for these

ISBN 0-590-46162-1

10 9 8 7 6 5   5 6 7 8/9

Printed in the U.S.A.   40

First Scholastic printing February 1994

CONTENTS

INTRODUCTION:
LOOK UP!

Did you ever stare at the sky on a summer night and wonder if somewhere out in that vast and starry deep there were other beings like us? Intelligent creatures who dreamed of building ships that could cross the great emptiness of space? Beings from worlds so strange that we could scarcely imagine them? Beings who might come visit *us*?

I bet you have. I know I did when I was a kid. (I still do, as a matter of fact.) So have all the other writers in this collection. And from those wonderings and speculations have come these stories, tales of aliens fierce and funny, sad and strange, to tickle your imagination.

Stories about aliens have been around for a long time now. One of the first major ones was a novel called *The War of the Worlds*, a frightening tale about a Martian invasion of

Earth, written by the English author H. G. Wells. Of course, these days we've pretty much given up on the idea that there might be life on Mars—but not on the idea that we might someday be visited by hostile aliens. Mr. Wells's story set a pattern that was followed for a long time, an assumption that intelligent life from another planet would likely be terrible and hostile. Science fiction stories are filled with what came to be known as BEMs (short for "Bug-Eyed Monsters").

Though such stories strike many people as farfetched, in a way they simply reflect some of the fears of our society. At various times in this century we Americans have felt enormous anxiety about invasion from abroad; enormous fear that strange people with strange ideas wanted to take over our country. Many science fiction stories can be seen as metaphors for that fear.

But eventually another kind of alien began to appear in science fiction stories—the super-intelligent, *friendly* alien. After all, since *we* were not yet able to cross the distances of space, any creature that could come here must surely be more advanced than we are. Was it too much to hope, even *expect*, that a species that could achieve interstellar travel would also have achieved a higher level of behavior—even have given up war?

Introduction

Ever seeking new and exciting story ideas, science fiction writers have continually stretched their imaginations to create unique aliens—some menacing, some friendly, some simply curious about our strange planet.

Yet some critics suspect that the human mind can never create something that is truly alien. They say that the very fact that humans are doing the creating means the thing created will have human elements; that if we ever do meet aliens, they may well be stranger than anything we could possibly imagine.

That may be so. But reading stories such as you'll find in this book is one way to prepare for the day many of us dream about, the day some people think will never come and others think is inevitable—the day that we first meet life from beyond the stars and learn that we are indeed not alone in the universe.

So dig in. Have a good time. And the next time you're outside on a starry night—look up!

Who knows what might be out there, looking back?

BRUCE COVILLE'S
BOOK OF

If we go to other planets,
does that make us the aliens?

I, EARTHLING

Bruce Coville

It's not easy being the only kid in your class who doesn't have six arms and an extra eye in the middle of your forehead. But that's the way it's been for me since my father dragged me here to Kwarkis.

It's all supposed to be a great honor, of course. Dad is a career diplomat, and being chosen the first ambassador to another planet was (as he has told me more times than I can count) the crowning achievement of his career.

Me, I just want to go home—though to hear Dad tell it, Kwarkis *is* home. I'm afraid he's fallen in love with the place. I guess I can't blame him for that. What with the singing purple forests, the water and air being sparkling clean (which *really* makes me feel like I'm on another planet), and those famous nights with three full moons, this truly is a beautiful place.

But it's not home. The people aren't *my* people. And most of the time I just feel lonely and stupid.

According to Dad, the first feeling is reasonable, the second silly. "You've got cause to feel lonely, Jacob," he'll say, standing over me. "And I'm sorry for that. But you have *no* reason to feel stupid."

A fat lot he knows. He doesn't have to go to school with kids who can do things three times as fast as he can, because they have three times as many hands. Even worse, they're just basically smarter than I am. *All* of them. I am the dumbest one in the class—which isn't easy to cope with, since I was always one of the smartest kids back home.

I'll never forget my first day at school here. My father led me in and stood me next to Darva Preet, the teacher. She smiled that strange Kwarkissian smile, reached down one of her six arms to take my hand, then turned to the room and cried: "Class! Class! Come to order! I want you to meet our new student— the alien you've all heard so much about!"

I began to blush. It was still hard to think of myself as an alien. But of course, that's what I was: The only kid from Earth on a planet full of people that *I* had considered aliens until I got here. Now that I was on Kwarkis, the situation was reversed. Now *I* was the alien.

The kids all turned toward me and stared, blinking their middle eyes the way they do when they are really examining something. I stared back, which is what I had been taught to do on the trip here. After a moment one of them dug a finger into his nose, pulled out an enormous booger, then popped it into his mouth and began to chew. The sight made my stomach lurch, but I tried not to let my disgust show on my face. Fior Langis, the Kwarkissian diplomat who had been in charge of preparing me for this day, had taught me that Kwarkissians feel very differently about bodily functions than we do.

"Greetings," I said in Kwarkissian, which I had learned through sleep-tapes on my way here. "I am glad to be part of the class. I hope we will have good times together."

Everyone smiled in delight, surprised that I knew their language. Then they all farted in unison. The sound was incredible—a rumbling so massive that for a moment I thought a small bomb had gone off. I jumped, even though Fior Langis had warned me that this was the way Kwarkissians show their approval. What she *hadn't* told me about, prepared me for, was the tremendous odor.

3

My eyes began to water.

I had a hard time breathing.

I fell over in a dead faint.

When I woke, I was in the hospital.

Since then the kids have referred to me as *Kilu-gwan*, which means "The Delicate One." I find this pretty embarrassing, since I was one of the toughest kids in class back on Earth. It doesn't really make that much difference here on Kwarkis, where no one fights. But I don't plan to live here forever, and I'll need to be tough when I get home to Earth. Back there you have to be tough to survive.

The only one who doesn't call me Kilu-gwan is Fifka Dworkis, who is the closest thing I have to a friend here. Fifka was the first one who talked to me after my embarrassing introduction to the class.

"Do not worry about it, Jay-cobe," he said, pronouncing my Earth name as well as he could with his strange oval mouth and snake-like green tongue. "The others will not hold your oversensitive olfactory organ against you."

He put his arm around my shoulder. Then he put another arm around my ribs, and another one around my waist!

I tried not to squirm, because I knew he was just being friendly. But it sure felt *weird*.

To tell the truth, it wasn't just the

weirdness that bothered me. It was also that I felt pretty inadequate having only one arm to offer back. Kwarkissian friends are always walking down the street arm in arm in arm in arm in arm in arm, and I wondered if Fifka felt cheated, only getting one arm back.

Whether or not he felt cheated, he doesn't spend a lot of time with me. He's always kind when he sees me, but he has never stayed overnight, or anything like that. Sometimes I suspect that the reason Fifka is nice to me is that his mother has told him to be. She's part of the Kwarkissian diplomatic team that works with Dad.

The only real friend I have here is my double-miniature panda, Ralph J. Bear, whom I brought with me from Earth. In case you've been living on another planet (ha, ha) the new double-miniature breeds are only about six inches tall. Ralph can easily fit right in my hand.

I like to watch him strolling around my desk while I do my homework. (Yes, I still have homework; I guess some things are the same no matter where you go!) And he's so neat and clean that Dad doesn't object to my letting him eat off my plate at the table. I love him so much I can hardly stand it.

The Chinese ambassador gave me Ralph at the big going-away party the United Nations threw for Dad and me. The gift was a surprise to everyone, since the Chinese are still pretty much holding on to the miniatures.

(Of course, between the fact that there are so few of them available, and the fact that they are devastatingly cute, there is an enormous demand for them. People were wildly jealous of me for having Ralph, but I figure I ought to get *some* benefit from being a diplomat's son. I mean, none of those people who were so jealous about Ralph were being dragged off to live on another planet!)

As it turns out, Ralph is one reason that the Kwarkissians made contact with Earth in the first place. Well, not Ralph J. Bear himself. But the breeding program he came from was part of a major last-ditch effort to save the pandas. According to Dad, the Kwarkissians have been monitoring us for a long time. His contacts say that one thing that made them decide we were worth meeting was that we started taking our biosphere seriously enough to really work at saving endangered species, such as pandas.

Anyway, Ralph is the only real friend I have here. So you can imagine how horrified I was when I was asked to give him away.

"What am I going to do, Ralph?" I said, trying not to cry.

The genetic engineers who created the

miniatures have enhanced their intelligence, too. Ralph J. Bear is very bright, and he always knows when something is bothering me. Waddling across my desk, he stood on his hind legs and lifted his arms for me to pick him up.

I set him on my shoulder, and he nestled into my neck. Normally that would have made me feel a lot better. Now it had the reverse effect, because it only made me more aware of how much I would miss him if I had to give him away.

I've been avoiding talking about how I got into this mess, because it is so embarrassing, but I suppose I had better explain it if any of the rest of this is going to make sense.

It started while we were having a diplomatic dinner here at the house.

According to my father, diplomatic dinners are very important. He says much of the major work in his profession happens around dinner tables, rather than at office desks.

The big thing he is working on right now is a treaty that has to do with who gets to deal with Earth. See, what most people back home don't know yet is the Kwarkissians aren't the only ones out here. But since they were the first to make contact with us, according to the rules of the OSFR (Organization of Space-

Faring Races), they get to *control* contact with us for the next fifty years.

My father was not amused when he found this out. He thinks the Kwarkissians shouldn't be able to do that. He feels they're treating Earth like a colony, and that it should be *our* choice who has contact with us. But he doesn't want to make the Kwarkissians angry. For one thing, they've been very good to us. For another, we suspect they could probably turn us (by "us" I mean the entire planet) into cosmic dust without much trouble.

So the situation is very touchy.

Dad is dealing with this other planet called—well, I can't actually write down what it's called, because no one ever says the name; it's against their religion, or something. Anyway, this planet that shall remain nameless is interested in making contact with us. But to do so they have to go through the Kwarkissians.

Dad is all in favor of it; he says the more trading partners Earth has, the better. So he was throwing this dinner, where we were going to get together with a bunch of Kwarkissians, including Fifka's mom, and a bunch of dudes from the nameless planet, including their head guy, whose name is Nnnnnn.

Dad asked me to be part of the dinner group because (a) people usually want to meet your kids, no matter what planet you come from, and, besides, (b) it's good diplomacy, because it usually softens people up. I know Dad feels a little guilty about using me like this, but I tell him not to, since I'm glad to be of some help—especially here on Kwarkis, where I feel like such a doof.

Diplomatic dinners are always a little tricky because you want to keep from offending anyone, which is not so easy when you have people from three different cultures sitting down to eat together. This is true even on Earth, so you can imagine what it was like for us to have representatives not from three countries, but three *planets.*

"Look, this is going to be a delicate situation," said Dad. "The Kwarkissians want to have you around tonight. They were quite insistent on it, in fact; they're very fond of you, you know. But Nnnnnn and his group don't like children—partly because in their culture childhood barely exists."

"What do you mean, 'childhood barely exists'?"

Dad frowned. "On Nnnnnn's planet children are hatched. They come out of the egg looking much like two-year-olds do on Earth, and mature very rapidly thereafter. Even with that, they're pretty much kept out of sight by their nurses and teachers until they're ready to join adult society. On Nnnnnn's world someone who looks as old as you do might well have gained adult status, which is a thing they take very seriously. They are going to consider you not as a child, but as an equal—so for heaven's sake be careful."

He handed me a computer printout on their culture and told me to read it. "There's a lot here you should know," he said. "Study it. The main thing to remember is, whatever else you do, don't compliment them on anything they show you."

He got up to leave the room. Stopping at the door, he added, "You'd better keep Ralph locked up for the night, too."

Then he told me how he wanted me to dress, and hurried off to tend to some details for the dinner.

I don't know about you, but when someone hands me something and tells me to read it, my mind immediately starts thinking of other things I need to do instead. It's not that I didn't want to learn about the new aliens; it's just that my brain rebels at being told what to do. So I put the printout aside and started to do something else.

A few minutes later my message receptor beeped. I pushed the Receive button, and a holographic image of Fifka, about four inches tall, appeared in the center of my desk. Ralph skittled away in surprise—he still hadn't gotten used to the Kwarkissian version of a phone call. I pushed the Send button so that Fifka could see me as well.

We started to talk about the dinner. He was excited because his mom was coming. I almost got the feeling he was jealous of her. That surprised me. When I thought about it, I realized that I had never actually invited Fifka to come visit; I had only thought about it, and waited for a good opportunity. Maybe he was more genuinely friendly than I had thought.

We got talking about something that had happened at school, and then about a game we were both working on, and by the time we were done I had pretty much forgotten about the printout Dad had given me. Next I did a little homework. Then I spent some time fooling around with Ralph J. Bear.

Before I knew it, it was time to get dressed.

That was when I noticed the printout lying on my bed.

I sighed. The thing had to be twenty pages long. No time to read that much before dinner. I would just have to be on my best behavior.

The flaw in that plan, of course, was that what one culture considers good behavior can get you in a lot of trouble somewhere else. . . .

* * *

I, Earthling

The dinner party consisted of Dad, me, three Kwarkissians (including Fifka's mother), and three beings from the planet that shall remain nameless. These guys only had two arms, which was sort of a relief, but they were bright green and seven feet tall.

The first part of the dinner went pretty well, I thought, if you set aside the fact that eating dinner with a bunch of Kwarkissians is like going to a symphony in gas-minor.

I had had a long talk about this with Fifka one day.

"Biology is biology," he said. "I hope this won't offend you, Jay-cobe, but most of us feel that if your people paid more attention to ideas and less to biological by-products, you would all be better off. After all, the important choices have to do with the mind and the heart, not the stomach and the intestines."

When he put it that way, it was hard to answer.

Still, it was a strange thing to sit down to dinner with some of the most important people on the planet and have them punctuate their conversation with gaseous emissions.

I had no idea how the guys from the planet that dares not speak its name were taking all this, since they barely talked at all. But they've been dealing with the Kwarkissians for centuries, so presumably they cope with it just fine.

The real trouble started *after* dinner, when we all went into the water room for dessert.

Every home on Kwarkis has a water room. It's one of my favorite things about living here. Basically it's a huge room with a multi-level stone floor. Clear water runs down one wall then flows through stream beds into the pools and ponds that dot the floor. There are even a few small waterfalls. Some of the ponds have fish—well, they're not really fish, but that's close enough. Also, there are a lot of plants and a few flying things that are sort of like birds.

The Kwarkissians spend a lot of their free time in the water rooms; they're a great place to chat and relax.

Well, we went there for dessert—at least, Dad and I were having dessert (gooey chocolate pie, to be precise). The Kwarkissians were chewing purple leaves, which was what they liked to do after dinner. The guys from Planet X were just sort of watching us. I got the impression they didn't do much of anything for fun on that planet.

While we were sitting there, Ralph J. Bear wandered in. I flinched, remembering that Dad had told me to keep Ralph in my room that night. I glanced at Dad. He didn't seem upset, but this didn't give me any useful information; Dad's training as a diplomat makes him *very* good at masking his real feelings. Certainly his face gave me no clue as to the kind of trouble I was about to get myself into.

When our guests saw Ralph they all wanted to pick him up—which seems to be an almost universal reaction to the little guy. At Dad's suggestion, I showed him around. Everyone liked him; even the guys from the planet with a secret name seemed to lighten up at the sight of him.

A little while later Nnnnnn tucked one long green hand under his robe and pulled out something that looked like a picture frame, the kind that you can open like a book. He opened it, looked inside, nodded, smiled in a sad kind of way, then started to pass it around. Each person who looked into it first appeared startled, and then—well, a strange look would cross his or her face. Sometimes it was happy, sometimes sad, but in all cases it was intense.

I couldn't wait for it to come to me.

I was sitting next to Fifka's mother. I had taken off my shoes, and we both had our legs dangling in the water. (Kwarkissians don't wear shoes, since the soles of their two-toed feet are like leather.)

When the thing the nameless-planet-guys were passing around came to Fifka's mom she looked into it and sighed. Then she passed it on to me.

Dad moved forward, as if to stop me from

taking it, then settled back against the mossy stone on which he was sitting. He looked worried, a slight slip in his diplomatic mask. That should have been a warning to me. But I was too eager to see what was inside the frame, so I ignored the expression on his face.

Big mistake.

Taking the frame, I opened it, and cried out in shock when I saw my mother looking out at me. Mom had died six years earlier, in a brush war in Asia she had been covering for *The New York Times*, and I mostly tried not to think about her, because it hurt too much. Now she was smiling at me as if she had never been gone.

I closed my eyes.

"The heartmirror sends a signal that generates an image from the brain," said Nnnnnn. "It pulls from the mind that which is deeply buried—that which you love, or fear, or wish most to see. What you see in the frame comes from yourself."

I opened my eyes again. My mother's face was still there, smiling at me. "It's wonderful," I said.

Nnnnnn's eyes narrowed in his green face. He made a sharp gesture, almost as if he were angry. "It is yours," he said gruffly.

My stomach tightened as I remembered Dad's warning: "Don't compliment them on anything they show you."

Suddenly I wished I had read that printout. What had I just done?

The room was silent, a heavy kind of silence that I found very frightening.

"Thank you," I said at last, nodding toward Nnnnnn.

More silence, then Nnnnnn said, "Your pet is wonderful, as well."

"Thank you," I said again.

For a time the only sound in the room was that of the water rolling down the wall, across the floor. The tension among the beings who sat around me was distinctly uncomfortable. I got the sense that they were waiting for something. I also had an idea *what*, but I tried to convince myself that I was wrong.

Finally Fifka's mother leaned over and whispered, "Nnnnnn is waiting for you to offer him your pet."

I felt as if she had hit me in the stomach.

Nnnnnn just sat there, staring at me.

Jumping up, I grabbed Ralph and ran from the room.

I was lying on my bed, holding Ralph and staring up through my ceiling—which I had set on "clear"—when my father came in. His face was dark with anger.

I ignored him and continued to stare at the

moons. They were all out, one at full, two in the crescent stage.

"Jacob, did you read that printout?" he asked.

I shook my head. A tear escaped from the corner of my eye. I was half embarrassed at crying, half hopeful that it might get me out of this mess.

Dad sighed.

"Why can't we just give Nnnnnn back the heartmirror?" I asked, trying to fight down the lump in my throat.

"If we do that, it will mark us as unworthy trading partners. Jacob, we have to follow through on this. It is a matter of honor for Nnnnnn and his people."

"So you want me to give Ralph to this guy just because he thinks I'm an adult and I got caught in some weird ritual that I didn't even know was going on? Forget it!"

I had overplayed my hand.

"If you had read the information I gave you, you would have been well aware of the custom," Dad snapped back. "Even ignoring that, you knew you were supposed to keep Ralph in your room. If you had done as I asked, none of this would have happened!"

He had me. I decided the best tactic was to ignore that fact and move on.

"Well, they can just go back to the nameless place they came from," I said defiantly. "I'm not giving Ralph to Nnnnnn. For all I know the guy just wants to eat him!"

Ralph whined and snuggled closer, and I felt a twinge of guilt. No one is sure just how much human language the little guys can understand. I hoped I hadn't scared him.

"Jacob, listen to me. Forging a good relationship with Nnnnnn and his group is—well, it could be a matter of life and death. The implications for Earth are overwhelming, and we simply can't afford a diplomatic incident right now. I'm sorry, but I have to insist. . . ."

I knew he meant it.

I also knew that I was not going to give Ralph to some weirdo from a nameless planet.

Which meant I also knew what I *was* going to do.

I remembered what Fifka had said about the important choices, that they had to do with the mind and the heart.

My mind and my heart were both telling me the same thing right now. I didn't like what they were saying, but when I thought about it, it wasn't a choice at all. Running away was my only option.

The trees were singing their night song as I slipped into the forest. The sky was darker now because the full moon had set, leaving only the two partial moons.

A buttersnake slithered around the base of one of the trees and stared at me in astonishment. It wasn't really a snake, of course—that's just what Dad and I call them. They're bright yellow, and can spread themselves out so flat they look like melted butter. They can go from flat to round in a half second when they are startled or angry. I tried not to make this one angry.

Ralph J. Bear clung to my neck, looking around with bright eyes and whimpering once or twice when shadows moved too close to us.

"It's all right, Ralph," I whispered. "We'll find someplace where we can hide until this blows over. Or maybe we'll hide out forever," I added, thinking that I couldn't see any good reason to go back at this point. I was tired of being the alien, the weird one, the outcast.

I remembered Toby, and wondered if this was how he had felt.

Toby had been the dumbest kid in my class, back in the last school I had been in before Dad and I moved to Kwarkis. He was okay, but he just wasn't with it. Some of the kids were mean to him, which I thought was stupid. Most of us pretty much ignored him.

I felt bad about that now. I wanted to go

back and put an arm around him, the way Fifka had put three arms around me, and tell him that I liked him. Which was true, now that I thought about it. He was a nice kid and never did anything to hurt anyone. I had always figured he didn't add anything to the class. I realized now that just his being there had been important. He was part of who we were, and we would have been different without him.

I wondered how the kids in Darva Preet's class felt about me. Did they think about me at all? Would they miss me, now that I was gone—or would they just be relieved that they didn't have a two-armed gimp around to deal with anymore? Did I make the class more or less than it had been when I came to it?

I was so wound up in my thoughts that I hardly noticed where I was going, hardly noticed Nnnnnn standing in my path until I almost bumped into him.

"Do you think this is wise?" he asked, his voice deep and solemn. He didn't sound mean, but there was something very frightening about him. I think it was simply that he was so sure of himself.

I stared at him, unable to speak.

He knelt in front of me and looked directly into my eyes.

"Are you an adult, or are you a child?" he asked.

My throat was dry, my stomach tightening into a knot of fear and despair. I remembered what my father had told me about the way Nnnnnn and his people felt about kids. Running away was one thing. Without me around Dad might have been able to skinny his way out of the mess I had created. (Though when I thought about it, I realized he would have turned that forest inside out to find me, no matter what it meant to the deal.) But face-to-face defiance of a diplomat from another planet was something else altogether.

The silence lay thick between us. Nnnnnn continued to stare into my eyes. I realized that there was no way I could lie to him.

"Are you an adult, or are you a child?" he repeated.

I swallowed hard, then told him the truth. "I'm both."

Nnnnnn nodded, which seemed to mean the same thing on his planet as on ours. "I suspected as much. Come with me."

He turned and walked away. I could have run in the other direction, but I didn't. I followed him.

We left the forest. The purple trees were singing the song they sing when the sky is clear. I cradled Ralph in my arms.

Nnnnnn led me to the bank of a stream. We sat and looked up at the stars.

I knew what he was showing me, or at least I thought I did. He was showing me the community that Earth might be invited to join, if I didn't screw things up.

Are you an adult, or are you a child?

The question burned in my ears. My father had given me the printout. He had told me to keep Ralph in my room. He had warned me not to compliment our guests on anything they showed us.

Every bit of the trouble I was in now was my own fault.

"Will you take good care of Ralph?" I asked, my voice thin and whispery, like dry leaves sliding against one another.

Nnnnnn was silent for a moment. At first I thought he was trying to decide how to answer the question. Later, I realized he was debating whether to answer it at all.

Finally he nodded. "I will," he said.

Trying hard not to cry, to keep the part of me that was an adult in charge, I lifted Ralph from my neck. Pressing him to my cheek, I wiped my tears against his fur, then passed him to Nnnnnn.

I wanted to say, "You don't know what this means." I wanted to say, "I am so lonely, and he is my closest friend." I wanted to say, "I hate you."

I said nothing.

Nnnnnn took Ralph from my hands. He placed him in his lap and stroked his fur. The water rippled past Nnnnnn's green feet. The stars filled the sky, the clear sky of Kwarkis, in an abundance we never see through the soiled air of Earth.

"Over there, that way, is my home," said Nnnnnn. "It is a sacred place, of great beauty. I do not like to be away from it."

I wondered why he was telling me this, then realized that it was a kind of gift. In saying this he was speaking to me as one adult to another.

He turned to look directly at me. "We have things that will bring your world much benefit, Jacob—things of beauty, things of value. We have medical technology, for example, that will mean that many who might have died in the next year will live instead."

I thought for a moment. "If I had known that, I would have given you Ralph without so much fuss. I would have hated you for it, but I would have given him to you."

"Of course you would have. That was not the issue. We are a trading race. It was not your compassion for your own kind that mattered

to us—it was your honor. Can we trust you?
That was what we needed to know."

"Can you?" I asked, my voice small. "I had
to be pushed."

He stopped me. "Your impulses are good,"
he said softly.

We sat in silence for a moment. Finally
Nnnnnn moved his green hand in a circle, indi-
cating the stream, the forest, the city. "I know
you feel like an alien here," he said softly. "But
that is because you are thinking too small. Yes,
you are from another world. So am I. If we
think of ourselves only as citizens of those
worlds, then here we are indeed the aliens. But
think in larger terms, Jacob." Now he swept
his hand in a half circle across the sky. "Look
at the grandness of it. You are a part of that,
as well. Your planet, my planet, Kwarkis—they
are all a part of something bigger. If you think
in terms of planets, then here you will always
be an alien. But you and your people can be
more, if you choose. You can be citizens of the
universe. If you see yourself that way, you will
never be an alien, no matter where you go. You
will simply be—one of us."

Lifting Ralph from his lap, he handed him
back to me.

I looked at him.

"It was not necessary that I *have* the ani-
mal," he said. "What was important was that

you fulfill your responsibility to me. I am glad that you did. It will mean much for your world."

He put his hand on my shoulder.

Ralph snuggled into the crook of my arm and went to sleep.

The stars shimmered above us.

I stared out at them, wondering how many I would visit.

Will Shetterly first wrote this story for his nephew (who also happens to be named Brian). When I found out he was working on it, I asked him to send me a copy. I'm glad he did. I bet you will be, too. . . .

BRIAN AND THE ALIENS

Will Shetterly

A boy and his dog were walking in the woods when they saw a spaceship land. Two space aliens came out of it. One alien was blue, and one was green, and they were both covered with scales, large red eyes, and long tentacles. Otherwise, there was nothing unusual about them.

The aliens walked into the middle of the clearing and jammed a flagpole into the ground. The flag had strange colors on it that hurt the boy's eyes, and odd lettering that looked like "We got here first. Nyah-nyah."

The boy whispered to his dog, "I'm not scared. You go first."

The dog said, "Rowf! Rowf!"

The boy thought the dog meant, "You are, too, scared. You can't fool me." So the boy said, "Am not," and he walked toward the aliens.

(What the dog really meant was, "If you'd throw a stick, I'd chew on it until it was soft and slimy, and then I'd bring it back so you could throw it again.")

The blue alien said, "Hello, native person. I am Miglick and this is my partner, Splortch. We have discovered your planet."

"Yep," said the green alien. "We did. It's ours."

"And we name it Miglick Planet," said Miglick.

"Yep," said Splortch. "We do. No, wait! We name it Splortch Planet."

The boy said, "It has a name. It's Earth."

Miglick told Splortch, "Perhaps we should name it for our home. We could call it New Veebilzania."

"Boring!" said Splortch.

"Everybody calls it Earth," said the boy.

"Rowf! Rowf!" said the dog.

Splortch said, "Are these Splortchians trying to tell us something?"

Miglick said, "The little Miglickian said 'Rowf!' I believe that means they'd like to give us all their gold." (What the dog really meant was, "Are these aliens friendly? Do they want to roll in some mud?")

"Um, we don't have any gold to give you," said the boy.

"That's too bad." All of Miglick's eyes squinted. "Then what were you saying, Miglickian?"

"My name's Brian. And I'm a human on Earth. This is Lucky. He's a dog."

"His name's Pry-on," Splortch told Miglick. "He's of the tribe of Splortchians called hummings. This clearing where we landed is called Urp. The little Splortchian is extremely fortunate. Its tribe are called ducks."

"I know that," said Miglick. "I heard everything the Miglickian said."

"No, you didn't," said Brian. "The entire planet is called *Earth*. The people who live on it are called *humans*. My name's *Brian*, his name's *Lucky*, and he's a *dog*. Okay?"

Most of Splortch's eyes squinted in a frown. "Excuse me. If you want to name things, discover your own planet."

"But humans were here first," said Brian.

"Okay," said Miglick. "Whenever we can't think of a better name for something, we'll use the old humming name. Isn't that fair?"

"That's fair," said Splortch, squatting on its tentacles to look at Lucky. "You don't have much to say, do you, fortunate duck?"

Brian said, "Ducks fly. They have wings. Lucky's a *dog*."

All of Splortch's eyes squinted in a frown. "I understand, Pry-on. I'm not stupid." The alien leaned close to Lucky. "So, where are your wings, fortunate duck?"

Lucky licked Splortch's face.

Miglick said, "I think that means the duck would rather not fly just now, but it is grateful that we discovered Miglick Planet."

Splortch looked at Brian. "You may lick my face, too, Pry-on."

Brian said, "No way!"

Miglick said, "The humming does not think it is worthy to lick your face."

Splortch said, "Ah, modest humming, you are indeed worthy to lick my face."

Brian shook his head. "Excuse me, but I don't want to lick anybody's face."

All of Splortch's eyes opened wide to stare at Brian. "Does that mean you aren't grateful that we discovered your planet?"

"Well," said Brian, "I always knew where it was."

Miglick sighed. "These Miglickians are so unreasonable. And to think I was sorry that they would all have to die."

"Have to what?" said Brian.

"Die," said Splortch. "You breathe oxygen, right?"

"Right," said Brian.

"Okay, then," said Miglick.

"Okay, then, what?" said Brian.

"Okay, then, you'll all die when we replace Earth's oxygen with methane," said Miglick. "Isn't that obvious?"

"Oh, dang," Brian said.

Splortch said, "Veebilzanians breathe methane. We took oxygen-breathing pills when we landed, but they don't last very long. And they taste terrible."

Brian said, "I don't want to seem rude or anything, but why do you have to replace our oxygen with methane?"

Splortch looked at Brian, then shrugged several tentacles and said, "What kind of rest stop would Splortch Planet be if Veebilzanians had to breathe oxygen? Can you imagine being cooped up in a spaceship for hours and hours and hours, and finally you come to a planet where you can get out and walk around, and there's no methane to breathe?"

Miglick looked at Splortch. "Inconceivable."

"But Earth isn't a rest stop," said Brian.

"Of course not," said Miglick. "Until we replace the oxygen."

"These Splortchians aren't very smart," said Splortch.

"No," said Miglick. "Well, let's start the methane-making machine."

"Wait!" shouted Brian. "You can't just kill everything on Earth."

"Sure we can." Splortch pointed at a control panel on the side of the spaceship. "We just press the red button. That starts the methane-making machine. Presto, Earth's a rest stop, and everyone's happy."

"But what about humans and dogs and everything that's already here?" asked Brian.

Miglick nodded. "The humming's right."

Splortch nodded, too. "Well, they won't be happy. They'll be dead." Splortch extended a tentacle toward the red button.

"Don't do that!" shouted Brian. "It's wrong!"

"It is?" Splortch drew its tentacle back to scratch its head. "It's not the green button, because that starts—"

"No," said Brian. "It's wrong to kill people."

"Hey, we know that." Miglick reached to press the red button.

"Don't!" shouted Brian. "Humans are people, too!"

"You are?" All of Splortch's eyes opened wide.

Brian nodded.

Splortch said. "Do you speak Veebilzanian?"

"Well, um, no," said Brian.

"Do you worship the great Hoozilgobbler?" said Miglick.

"Um, I don't think so," said Brian.

"You *don't* have tentacles," said Splortch.

"Well, no," Brian agreed. "But we're still people."

"Hmm," said Miglick. "Do you have spaceships that can travel between the stars?"

"We have space shuttles that can go around the Earth. And humans have been to the moon."

"Only to your moon?" Miglick laughed. "That's not a spaceship. That's a space *raft*."

"We're really people," said Brian. "If you got to know us, you'd see."

Splortch and Miglick glanced at each other. Miglick said, "This planet would make such a nice rest stop."

"True," said Splortch. "But hummings and ducks *might* be people."

"Quite right," said Miglick. "We'll have to find out."

"Whew!" said Brian, thinking the aliens would become someone else's problem now.

"Rowf!" Lucky said. (What Lucky meant was, "Does anyone want to go home and see if there's any brown glop in my food bowl? If there is, we can all get down on the floor and eat together.")

Splortch said, "You two Splortchians stand over there. We'd like to take your image."

"Our picture?" said Brian.

"I guess so," said Splortch.

Brian shrugged and led Lucky under a tree, where he stood looking at Splortch and Miglick, who were standing in front of the spaceship. Miglick said, "Perfect," and Brian smiled as the alien pressed the green button on the control panel.

In the next instant Brian was looking at a boy who looked exactly like himself and a dog who looked exactly like Lucky. The blue alien was standing beside Brian, and the green alien was missing. The tree was behind the boy and the dog, and the spaceship was behind Brian and the blue alien.

Brian said, "Hey! What happened?"

The blue alien said, "Rowf! Rowf!"

Brian raised a green tentacle to scratch his head, and then he stared at the tentacle.

The dog said, "Ret's go, Sprortch. And you two hummings, be carefur in our bodies."

"Don't press any buttons while we're gone," said the boy. "You don't want to start the methane machine until we're back."

Brian stared, then shook his tentacles in frustration.

"Rowf!" The blue alien rubbed its head

35

against Brian's tentacles until Brian patted it. "Rowf!"

"Rots o' things smell grr-reat!" said the dog.

"Come on, Miglick," said the boy. "The sooner we prove hummings aren't really people, the sooner we can start the methane-making machine."

"Rokay! See you rater!" The dog ran ahead of the boy to get a good whiff of a dead skunk. "Yo! That's grr-reat!"

"Dang!" Brian stomped his tentacles twice, and then he squatted and told the blue alien beside him, "It's okay, Lucky. We'll fix this. Um, somehow."

Just then, a woman behind him said, "All right, who's making a monster movie?"

Brian turned around. A tall police officer stood at the edge of the clearing with her hand on her holstered pistol.

Brian said, "I'm not a monster, I'm a space alien. I mean, I'm a kid, and this is my dog. No one's making a movie. Can you help?"

The police officer cocked her head to one side, then called, "Jack, what do you think?"

A fat police officer came out of the woods and walked toward the spaceship. He stared at it and said, "I think I don't know what I think, Sarge."

"It's simple," said Brian. "Only I can't explain it. And there's no time to try, 'cause we have to save Earth right away!"

"You're a kid?" The policewoman moved her hand away from her pistol and scratched her head.

"Sure," said Brian. "The aliens switched bodies with us by pushing that green button." He pointed at it with a tentacle.

"This one?" the policeman asked. And he pressed the green button.

Meanwhile, the alien who looked like Lucky and the alien who looked like Brian walked out of the woods. A girl called, "Brian!"

"Herro," said the dog.

"No, I think I'm Pry-on," said the boy. He called to the girl, "Who are you, humming from Urp?"

"What's the game?" said the girl.

"There's no game," said the boy. "I'm Splortch. This is Miglick. We're from Veebil-zania. We must decide whether we should kill everyone on your planet by turning it into a rest stop for space travelers."

The dog nodded in agreement.

"Okay," said the girl. "I'm Captain Brandi of the Starship *Enterprise*."

"Glad to meet you, Captain Pran-dee."

The girl said, "I've got your spaceship locked in a tractor beam. You have to leave

Earth alone, or I'll blow up your ship with my photon torpedoes."

"Oh, oh!" said the dog.

The girl said, "Is Lucky okay?"

The boy said, "Um, we have to go now."

"No way," said the girl. "Or I'll blow up your ship. Besides, Mom said you have to come in for lunch."

The boy said, "These Urp creatures are more clever than we suspected. Maybe they really are people."

"I don' know," said the dog.

The girl patted the dog's head. "Poor Lucky. Did you eat something you shouldn't have?"

A woman stepped out of a house and called, "Brian! Brandi! Lunch is ready!"

"Coming, Mom!" The girl grabbed the boy's hand and tugged him toward the house. The dog stared at them, then back at the woods, and then followed the girl and the boy inside.

At the kitchen table the girl sat in one chair, so the boy sat in another. The dog jumped into a third. The Mom looked at the dog and said, "Down, Lucky!"

"But he's hungry," said the boy.

"He has food." The Mom pointed at Lucky's dish, which was full of brown mush.

"Good!" said the dog as it jumped down.

"Lucky sure sounds strange," said the Mom.

"He can't speak as well as I can," said the boy. "And he can't pick up things in his hands." The boy pointed at his thumb. "I think it's because hummings have this special finger, and ducks don't. Tentacles are far more practical. And far more attractive."

The girl and the Mom laughed. The girl said, "Brian's a space alien. I always knew it."

The boy nodded proudly. "I am Splortch from Veebilzania. That is Miglick, my partner."

"Herro," said the dog, looking up from his dish.

"How do you like the duck food?" asked the boy.

"Good!" said the dog.

The Mom asked, "How'd you train Lucky to bark like that?"

"He di'n't," said the dog.

"I didn't," said the boy. "We learned your language from your television broadcasts."

The Mom put her hand on the boy's forehead. "I think you've been watching too much television, mister. Do you feel all right?"

Before the boy could answer, someone pressed the door buzzer. "I'll get it!" the girl said.

"Oh," said the boy in relief. "That's *not* the sound of you hummings blowing up our spaceship?"

The girl opened the front door, then said, "Mom? It's the police."

"No, it's not." A fat policeman walked into the room. "It's me, Brian."

"Rowf," said a tall policewoman, trotting in after the policeman.

"Oh, oh," said the boy.

"Ro, ro," said the dog.

"Mom!" said the policeman, pointing at the boy and the dog. "They're aliens and they want to kill everyone on Earth. We have to stop them!"

As the policewoman ran toward the dog dish, the policeman called, "Lucky! Come back here!" The policewoman barked sadly and returned to the policeman's side.

The Mom looked from the two police officers to the boy and the dog.

"It's me, really!" the policeman said. "The aliens switched bodies with Lucky and me. And when the police showed up, I got put into the policeman's body by mistake."

"That is not true," said the boy. "I'm Pryon the humming, not Splortch from Veebilzania." He pointed at the dog. "This is a fortunate duck, not my partner Miglick. Send away those hummings in blue clothing and let us stay with you until we decide whether you're really people."

The Mom stared at the boy.

The boy added, "Please?"

"Brian?" the Mom asked the boy. "The joke's over now, understand?"

"It's not a joke!" said the policeman. "If you don't believe me, they'll turn all the oxygen into methane, and everyone will die!"

"Yes, they're playing a joke!" said the boy. "But not me! I'm really Pry-on! Make the joking people go away!"

The Mom said, "This isn't funny, Brian." She turned toward the police officers. "And you two should be ashamed of yourselves, playing some game like this—"

The policewoman whimpered. The policeman said, "Oh, dang."

The girl pointed to the policeman. "Mom, that's Brian."

The woman stared at the boy. "Then who're you?"

"Oh, all right," said the boy, sighing. "I'm Splortch. I traded bodies with Pry-on."

The dog said, "But where are our real bodies?"

"Right here," said someone at the door.

"Hey, great!" said Brandi. "Space aliens!"

The green alien pointed a tentacle at the policewoman, who was hiding behind the policeman. "Just don't let me eat dog food, okay?"

"Don't worry, Sergeant," said the policeman. "Lucky does everything I tell him to—except when he doesn't."

At that moment a man in cowboy boots

walked in the front door and stared at the two aliens, the two police officers, the two children, the dog, and the Mom.

"Dad!" the policeman yelled, wrapping his arms around the surprised man and giving him a big hug. "You're home early!"

"Uh—" began the Dad.

"Roo's he?" said the dog.

The policewoman started drinking water out of Lucky's water dish.

The boy said, "Please tell Captain Pran-dee not to destroy our spaceship. We could put our rest stop on another planet."

"I—" began the Dad.

"Do you live here?" said the blue alien. "Or are you another space alien?"

"Um—" began the Dad.

"Everything's under control," the green alien said. "But your son promised he wouldn't let me drink out of the dog dish, and look at me now." The alien pointed a tentacle at the policewoman, who was happily lapping up water from the dog dish.

"Oh, sorry." The policeman released the very confused Dad and called, "Lucky! Stop that." The policewoman looked up from the dog dish, then ran over and crouched beside the policeman.

The Dad said, "If I go outside and come back in again, will this make sense?"

"I doubt it," said the Mom. "But if it works, I'll try it, too."

"We only saw your television broadcasts," said the boy. "We didn't know you were intelligent beings."

"Rat's right," said the dog. "We won't take away your grr-oxygen now."

The girl gave the Dad a hug. "Isn't this great? Everyone's in the wrong bodies, except for you and me and Mom!"

The blue alien said, "Sarge, I sure hope you'll write the report on this case," and then coughed.

The green alien nodded and said, "Maybe we should say we fell aslee—" and then coughed, too.

The Dad scratched his head. "This is one of those TV shows where they trick people, right?"

"No time to explain, Dad!" said the policeman, running outside with the policewoman following behind him. "C'mon, everybody!"

"Hey, our bodies!" cried the space aliens, running after the police officers.

"Hey, *our* bodies!" cried the boy and the dog, running after the aliens.

"Hey, Brian and Lucky!" cried the Dad, running after the boy and the dog.

"Hey, Dad!" cried the girl, running after the Dad.

"Hey, everybody!" cried the Mom, not

running after anyone. "Who's going to explain what's going on?"

"Not now, Mom!" said the policeman, stopping for a moment at the edge of the woods. "The aliens said their oxygen-breathing pills don't last very long!"

"Rat's right!" said the dog. "Grr-I forgot!"

"What oxygen-breathing pills?" asked the blue alien.

"I don't like the sound of this," said the green alien, and then it coughed again.

"Hurry!" said the girl, running back and grabbing the Mom's hand to lead her into the woods.

The Dad looked up into the trees as they ran. "They sure hide the video cameras well."

Just as everyone entered the clearing where the spaceship stood, the two aliens fell on the ground and began gasping desperately. The dog pressed a purple button on the spaceship's control panel, and two small yellow pills popped out. The dog gave them to the aliens. As soon as the aliens popped them into their mouths, they quit coughing.

After Splortch and Miglick used their machine to put everyone back into their proper bodies, Splortch said, "Thank you for not destroying our ship, Captain Pran-dee."

The girl shrugged. "Oh, that's all right."

Splortch said, "And thank you for remembering about the oxygen-breathing pills, Pry-on. You saved us from having to live the rest of our lives as hideous freaks. Um, nothing personal."

"I kind of liked being a duck," said Miglick.

"*I* kind of like being alive," said the policewoman. "You did good, kid."

Brian blushed and shrugged. "That's all right."

Splortch said, "After we build a rest stop on Pluto, you all have to come and visit us."

"That'd be nice," said the Mom.

"And bring some of that good duck food," called Miglick as the spaceship's door closed behind him.

"Goodbye!" everyone shouted as the spaceship took off. After it disappeared in the sky, the Dad said, "They use very long wires and a *really* big mirror, right?"

"Let's go finish our lunch," said the Mom.

Brian patted Lucky's head. "Glad to be a dog again?"

Lucky licked Brian's face and said "Rowf! Rowf!" And everyone knew that meant "Yes!" (Though it really meant "You smell that dead skunk? Let's all go roll on it!")

When aliens come looking for the best
we have to offer . . .

JUDGMENT DAY

Jack C. Haldeman II

They were coming.

I woke up knowing that, just as I knew they wouldn't take me. There are many things in my life I am ashamed of. They might take Laura, though. She's the one truly good person I know. I nudged her awake.

"I had the strangest dream," she said, sleepily brushing the hair from her face.

"I know," I said. "I had it too."

She looked at me with that half-awake way that she has. I could tell she understood.

"They won't take me either," she said. There was sadness in her voice.

"They might. You've never hurt anyone in your life. You're a kind and good person."

She shook her head. "I'm not good enough," she said. "Not for them."

It was true, and we both knew it in our hearts. They wanted perfection, nothing less.

Laura shivered, and I held her close. The bedroom was dark, and we shared a secret the whole world knew. I listened to the clock tick. There wasn't much to say. We stayed that way all morning, and I didn't go to work.

Everything stopped that day. No wars, no work, no play: it wasn't a day for that. Men and women around the world looked to the stars and into their hearts. They saw the darkness, the shortcomings. Each in his or her own way grieved for what man had become. It had come to this—all the promise, all the hopes. There was nothing to do but wait. They were coming.

The dream had a billion voices, and it touched us all. The powerful and the poor got the same message. When night had passed we all understood. Earth would have everything, or Earth would have oblivion. We would share the universe in peace and love with a thousand alien races, or we would be destroyed in an instant like an insect or some dread disease. It was their decision to make, and, before they chose, they wanted to examine a sample from our population.

They wanted the best.

It was fair, no one could dispute that. They weren't interested in the ones who held power, or the wisest, or the richest people in the world. They wanted the best that Earth had to offer. Nothing less would do. In the night that they touched our minds, they had also made their decision. There was nothing to do but wait for them to come and to see whom they had chosen.

It wouldn't be the smoothest talker who would speak for Earth. The wisest men wouldn't plead our case before the collective minds of a thousand planets. They weren't interested in words or great deeds. What they wanted was kindness, compassion. I wondered where they'd find it.

They were giving us the best chance that Earth could have. There would be no deceit, no lies, no misunderstandings. They would take two—they had chosen two—and these two would speak for Earth. There would be no others; there would be no second chance. We waited and wondered.

Everything stood still. Even the pulpits were quiet. What we had seen that night had made us look deep into our souls, and we all fell short. We looked at what we could have been and measured it against what we had become. It was a dark pain, and we all felt it.

Then they came.

They came in a silver ship and said nothing; there was nothing to say; they had said it all that night. Silently they went to those they had chosen, and then they left.

They took to the stars two dolphins, a mated pair.

We are waiting for their decision.

*Once you meet an alien, you'll never
be the same.*

THE BUDDY SYSTEM

Nina Kiriki Hoffman

Something in Miller's Pond grabbed my ankle, and it wasn't Kyle Ingleman.

Kyle and I had come through the sprinklers on summer lawns in the after-dinner dusk for our first summer vacation swim in Miller's Pond. We were thirteen and it was our fourth summer together as next-door neighbors and best friends, as buddies.

Mom had explained the buddy system to us the day Kyle and I met, two days after my ninth birthday. Kyle had wandered over to look at what was coming out of our little U-Haul. He was a thin boy with freckles and messy dark hair, and I thought he was beautiful, maybe even magic. Mom smiled at Kyle and accepted his help carrying boxes into our new bungalow, the smallest house we'd ever lived in, big enough now that Daddy had gone away.

After we'd gotten most of the boxes inside, Mom took us into the new kitchen and gave us Toll House cookies she had baked just before we packed the dishes at our old house. She said, "Kyle, will you be Iris's buddy? That means she watches out for you, and you watch out for her; you check up to make sure she's okay and not lost, and she does that for you."

Kyle stood up straighter and stared at me, his dark eyes serious, and at last he said, "Okay."

"Iris, will you be Kyle's buddy?" Mom asked me.

I felt squirmy, and mad at her—what if he'd said no? What if he thought it was stupid? I also felt happy because he had said yes. I stared at the linoleum and said, "Okay." I looked up at Mom. I knew she was sad because Dad used to be her buddy and now he wasn't around. I looked at Kyle. He still looked magic.

That was before Mom and I knew anything about him, except that he had helped us. I found out a lot more later, but it didn't change how I felt about him. He stole things from stores; sometimes he stole things from people at school, and from his brother and sister and his parents, but he never stole anything from me or Mom, even though that first day he had come over looking for things to steal. He never lied to us. He watched out for me.

The Buddy System

"Can you show Iris the special places in the neighborhood?" Mom had asked. "The safe places?"

So the day I moved in next door to Kyle, he showed me Miller's Pond, and from then on we spent most summer afternoons and evenings swimming there and exploring the woods around the pond.

None of the other kids swam there; they went to the municipal pool instead. Kyle's older sister said Miller's Pond was haunted. His younger brother said it was polluted. Kyle and I swam there and didn't get sick. Mom, who had been out to see the pond, said it was okay for us to swim there, since we'd both had swimming lessons, as long as we watched out for each other.

The first vacation night of our thirteenth summer was warm and moonless, stars shimmering smears against the dark gray-green-blue sky. The air smelled like walked-on weeds and tadpole water. Kyle and I dropped our towels on the grass, shucked out of our T-shirts, and slipped into the pooled dark. The water was still sun-warm near the surface, cooler down by my toes. I stretched out in the surface layer, stroking sideways and trying not to stir up the cold.

"What's that you're wearing?" Kyle said

after we had paddled out to the middle of the pond.

"A bikini." I hugged myself under water. All the previous summers I had worn cutoff jeans and a T-shirt in swimming; Kyle wore cutoffs and sometimes a T-shirt and sometimes not. Sometimes after we were in the water, I had taken my T-shirt off. But now I was growing.

Mom had taken me shopping the week before for bras and a new swimsuit. After the embarrassment of being fitted for a bra by a saleslady, I had felt angry and reckless, and had chosen . . .

A bikini. Terminally stupid. I could have worn a T-shirt and shorts, or even my old one-piece, which I still wore when we went to the public pool. Why did I wear the stupid bikini? Just because I bought it didn't mean I had to wear it. But I'd seen Kyle looking at Carol Hunnicutt in class, and I had thought . . .

"Hmm," said Kyle. He ducked underwater.

I ducked under, too, hoping the water would cool my burning cheeks. I swam a long way under water and came up over by the far side of pond.

"Iris?" Kyle was saying.

"Here," I said, because you had to, by buddy system rules.

"What are you doing over there?" he said.

"I—"

Something touched the arch of my foot. I wondered if it was a weed. It tickled me again and I decided not. I pulled my foot up against my thigh. "Kyle?"

"Yeah?" He was still twenty feet away.

Something curled tight around my other ankle, and I knew it wasn't Kyle. "Kyle!" I yelped. I kicked both legs, trying to break away from what had grabbed me or at least kick it.

All that happened was that it snagged my other ankle, too, and no matter how hard I kicked, I couldn't get loose. It didn't feel like hands around my ankles—more like smooth warm nooses. "Help! Something grabbed me!" I cried.

I heard Kyle stroking toward me. The ropes around my ankles didn't tighten or try to pull me down, but they didn't let go, either. Then something soft and sticky sucked up against the soles of my feet, and I screamed.

Kyle's swimming got more frantic. "Iris!" he yelled.

"Here!"

The soft sticky things moved like fingers against the bottoms of my feet. Then hot pins pricked the soles. I groaned. My feet tingled and burned. The heat traveled up my legs and spread out through my body, finally reaching my head. "Kyyyyllle," I said. My mouth didn't work right.

"What is it? What?" He grabbed my arm. "Come on!"

He tugged at me, but the nooses around my ankles held me firmly. Pulling against them hurt.

I had a sudden thought. There might be more nooses. My head felt hot, my tongue felt hot, my throat felt hot. I wasn't sure I could talk anymore, but Kyle was my buddy, and I had to warn him. I swallowed and said, "Get away, Kyle!"

"No!" He was still pulling on my hands and kicking, trying to tug me loose. The ropes around my ankles felt like they might slice through my legs.

"Stop it! Let go! Get away!"

My voice sounded deep and distorted, like a record played too slow. My brain was fizzing. Suddenly I couldn't see, hear, or feel anything.

It was a relief.

Gradually into the quiet darkness little glimmers of light bloomed, forming a dotted outline picture. At first I thought it was a picture of a stretched-out five-pointed star, but I realized that the top ray was round, not pointed, and the other rays had blobs on their ends, like fencing swords with buttons on the tips.

This is weird, I thought. I tried to blink. I didn't seem to have eyes.

The buttons on the upper two rays grew five fingers each. On the bottom two rays the blobs stretched out and sprouted toes.

It was a picture of a person, an outline of glowing yellow dots nobody had connected yet. I watched without eyes as light-dots fused and moved and the outline shaped itself more and more like the edges of a human.

Next to it a new picture formed, a central blob with a whole lot of skinny curvy rays going out in all directions, some longer, some shorter, a few fatter. It looked like a little kid's picture of a sun on a really bright day.

The blob-with-rays moved under the star-person's feet, and two of the blob's rays reached up and went around the star-person's ankles. Two of the shorter fat rays touched the feet.

I would have screamed or jumped if I could. All I wanted to do was head some other direction as fast as possible—get home to Mom, to Kyle, to safety. But I still had no sense of my body. I couldn't feel anything. I couldn't move.

The octoblob let go of the star-person's feet and moved up beside the star-person again, then reached out a ray. The star-person moved

its arm so that its hand touched the octoblob's
ray.

The picture faded.

Kyle was crying, his sobs like coughs,
when I opened my eyes.

It was still night, and I was lying on grass,
staring up at stars. All my muscles felt tired
and loose, and my bikini, still wet, made bands
of cold on my body. The last remnant of heat
washed away, and I started shivering.

"Kyle?" I croaked. My throat felt raw.

He coughed, his shoulders shaking, his
hands over his face. I lifted an arm. My muscles hurt the way they had after I arm-wrestled
every boy in my class. I touched Kyle's leg.

He dropped his hands and looked down at
me.

"Iris!" He grabbed me and hugged me so
hard I could barely breathe. "Iris! Jeeze! I
thought—"

"Let's go home," I whispered.

He had to half carry me, but we got there.

Mom took one look at our faces—I don't
know what mine looked like, but Kyle still
looked shocked and hurt and pale—and settled
us in blankets in the kitchen. She put water
on to heat. "What happened?" she asked.

"Something in the pond grabbed her," Kyle
said.

"What!"

"And I couldn't get her loose, and she blacked out and I was afraid she'd drown and I couldn't go for help because what if she drowned while I was gone? And she finally came loose, but when I got her up on the bank, she was barely breathing, and I tried artificial respiration because I couldn't think of anything else, even though she had a pulse and she was breathing, and I didn't think I could carry her back to the road, but I was afraid to go get help and leave her all alone, and I didn't know what to do and, and, and, finally she woke up. I'm sorry, Norma. I'm sorry, Norma."

"Iris, are you okay?" Mom said, her forehead worried into wrinkles, her voice anxious.

"I guess," I said. My throat hurt.

The teakettle whistled, and Mom made us peppermint tea, which helped my throat.

She said, "Do we need to take you to the hospital? Where does it hurt?"

I closed my eyes and thought about my body. "I just feel really tired," I said. "And . . ." I stretched my legs out from under the table and looked at my ankles. There were red bands around them. They didn't hurt as much now, but they tingled.

"What happened!" Mom said, staring.

"That's where it grabbed me," I said. "I

don't think it would be so bad if we hadn't been trying to pull away."

I lifted one of my feet up onto my thigh and looked at the sole. It was bright pink. I leaned over and looked hard, but I couldn't see any wounds. What had felt like pins and needles might just have been some kind of energy.

"It grabbed you? What grabbed you? I've never seen anything like this." Mom leaned over and touched the red mark on my ankle. Her fingertip felt fiery hot. I sucked in my breath between my teeth.

"I don't know," I said, my voice tight. I remembered the pictures I had seen, though. "I think we better not swim in Miller's Pond anymore."

Kyle and I were exhausted. Pretty soon he went home, and I went to bed. Mom hugged me hard when we said good night.

Even though I was really tired, I had a tough time falling asleep.

"Not to swim," I said again.

"You're crazy," Kyle said.

We were sitting on the living room floor, tearing pictures from out-of-date magazines Mom brought home from the waiting room of the medical complex where she worked. I loved pictures. Sometimes I cut them up and put together bigger pictures, but mostly I just gluesticked them to notebook paper and put them in three-ring binders. Mom had bought me a camera for my tenth birthday, and I had decided I was going to be a photographer when I grew up. I liked studying how other people took pictures.

Kyle took a picture of the Guess jeans guy and tore it into pieces. He knew I was collecting those.

"We don't have to get into the pond," I said. "We don't even have to dip our toes in. I just want to go look. It's broad daylight. What could happen?"

"What could happen?" he said in a choked voice. "How can we tell? I never thought you'd get caught the way you did! We're never going back there."

I cut out a picture of supermodel Paulina Porizkova. She's my favorite. "Mom went and put up a sign. She told the police it's not safe there. She asked them to see about putting up a fence. I have to go back before it gets fenced off, Kyle. If you won't come with me, I'll go alone."

"No! You are not going back there alone! Swear it. Cross your heart and hope to die, stick a needle in your eye. You won't go back there alone, not if you want to stay buddies."

I closed my eyes for a minute, feeling a tug on my heart, hearing a voice in my brain that whispered I had to go back to the pond. It felt like a hunger too strong to ignore. Then I looked at Kyle, feeling a thickening in my throat that made me wonder if it was swelling up like a frog about to croak. Being Kyle's buddy meant not being scared, not being lonely, having someone to talk to, share with, count on. I glanced at the floor, feeling heat behind my eyes. "I swear," I said at last, my voice half swallowed. I looked up.

He stared at me for a long time. "Okay, I'll go. You wait a minute, though. I have to get something from home."

While he was gone I picked up the magazines and put them in my storage cupboard with my binders and office supplies.

He came back with a buck knife.

"Whose is that?" I asked, breaking our unspoken pact; I never asked him about things he had.

"Dad's," he said. "I'll put it back. I just don't want something to grab you without me being able to stop it or at least cut you loose."

"Don't use it unless I ask you to," I said.

His eyes widened. He didn't make any promises.

We went to the end of our street and then up the track through the woods that led to the pond. There was a big white sign with black

letters right in front of the pond: BEWARE! DON'T
SWIM HERE! DANGER!

The pond lay quiet and dark and cool in
the hot afternoon sunlight. I went around to
the side where I had been when I was grabbed.
I sat on the bank, hugging my knees to my
chest. Kyle sat down beside me and took out
the knife. We stared at the water for a while.
It was clear at the edges, shading to green darkness in the center. On this side it got deep and
hard to see through very fast.

I thought about the pictures in my head. I
looked at Kyle.

"Okay," I said. "Put the knife away. Listen, I know what it was—it was some other
kind of person. It just wanted to talk. I know
it was scary, but I want to try talking again."

"What?" he said.

"I'm going to reach down and touch it
again," I said. "And I don't want you to hurt
it. I'll be okay. I got better last time, didn't I?"

"Iris . . ."

I lay on my stomach and rolled up my
sleeve. "Don't hurt it," I said, then stuck my
arm down in the water. I wiggled my fingers.

I could see the pebbles and rocks on the
bottom near the edge, dropping away into the
depths. Suddenly some of the pebbles shifted.
A thing like a snake or an eel lifted up. Its back
looked just like the pebbles and earth around

it. Its tail disappeared down into the darkness. Its head—more like an eyeless bulge—rose toward my hand.

For a second I wanted to jerk my hand up out of the water and run away. I held my free hand out to Kyle, and he gripped it. I glanced at him. He was staring down at the snake-thing. The knife sat by his knee, but he wasn't holding it.

The eyeless bulge turned over, showing a dense mass of frilly pale green tendrils, each about as long and thick as a mouse's tail. I gritted my teeth and reached to touch the tendrils. They felt soft and sticky, and they pressed heated pins against my palm and fingers. I closed my eyes, feeling the heat travel through me.

Immediately I went to the dark place of no sound or touch. The picture of the star-human and the octoblob holding hands was already there against the dark chalkboard. After a minute a lot of other little light-framed shapes pinpricked into being, and the octoblob touched each of them with a different tentacle. Some of them looked like the outlines of fish, trees, birds. Some of them looked like microorganisms I had seen in my science textbook. Some I couldn't tell what they were.

Then the whole image joggled sideways and slipped away, as my hand went cold. I was back in my own head, looking out at sky, woods, pond. Kyle was lying beside me, reaching down. His hand had edged mine aside. I thought he was going to stab the tentacle, but the knife was still on the grass between us. He touched the sticky side of the tentacle. Then all the muscles in his arm went tight, his eyes widened, and his mouth dropped open. He stared, frozen, at nothing.

Was that what I had looked like? If I had seen him do it first, I don't know if I would have had the courage to reach for the tentacle myself.

I pressed my hand against the sea-anemone surface next to Kyle's. The little soft sticky tendrils moved against my hand again, strobing heat, and I was back in pictureland. There were so many glowing dots sprinkled on the surface in front of me it was hard to sort them into things. After a while I could see that two star-people touched hands to tentacles with the octoblob.

I wondered if I could make pictures, too. I concentrated, thinking of images that weren't photographs or even paintings, but constellations. I imagined a second octoblob outlined in light. Presently weak pinpricks of light shone in a little circle below the other images, with rays of pinpricks leading from the circle, one of the rays touching a tentacle of the octoblob.

My lights shone pale green-blue instead of yellow, and the lines wavered. Still, I was amazed that I could get lights to show up at all.

My picture of a second octoblob glowed green for a minute. Then I felt something shift, like threads snipped by scissors, and it faded. The original octoblob waved two tentacles at it as if saying goodbye.

I imagined the first star-person, the one that meant me, letting go of the octoblob's tentacle. Its hand lifted after I thought about it. Then I was back in the real world, my hand free. I pushed up from the bank and sat. Kyle was still frozen, slack-jawed, hand in the water.

This time I didn't feel tired or sick. I guessed most of the hurt of the first encounter was from struggling to get away.

After a while Kyle slumped and blinked and closed his mouth. He stared up at me. He pulled his hand out of the water and sat up beside me. The tentacle turned over and disappeared against the bottom.

"Did you hear it?" Kyle whispered.

"Hear it? I saw pictures. What did you hear?"

"It was telling a story, but in music, and I couldn't understand it very well. But—" He rubbed his eyes. "I think it was sad."

"I think it's alone," I said, remembering

the way my suggestion of another octoblob had been erased.

"Yeah," he said. "In the story—it was weird, because it was all harps and flutes, and then this thin guitar riff came in trying to play the same tune but not quite in key, and then it disappeared—"

My octoblob picture, I thought: *I tried to make it look like the first octoblob, but it didn't.*

"—and the story was about how there are so many things on Earth and this thing is listening to all of them. All alone."

"Now it's listened to us," I said.

"Yeah," he said quietly. "What do we do about it?"

"Nothing," I said. "Except maybe listen to it back. And let it listen to us some more."

Listening wasn't the right word. I thought of the pinprick pictures. Looking? The sticky hot-needle feel of it against my hand. Touching?

Communicating?

By the time Mom gave up trying to convince the city council to build a fence around Miller's Pond a couple weeks later, the octoblob had gone. Kyle and I didn't see it go; we just went there one day and stuck our hands in the water and nothing rose up to touch us back. So we sat up and held each other's hands and tried to make the music and pictures between us—we had learned that while connected to the octoblob, we could talk in the octoblob's language, Kyle in music that I saw as pictures, and I in pictures that Kyle heard as music—but nothing happened, except our hands got hot and sweaty and I felt anxious and fluttery and finally Kyle kissed me.

Eventually we went home. I got out my construction paper and my scissors. Kyle sat down at Mom's spinet piano. While I cut yellow and green-blue circles out and pasted them to a dark gray background, Kyle noodled on the piano with one finger.

By the time Mom came home from work, I had done six pictures, the last one looking a lot like the lights I'd seen while touching the octoblob's tentacles, and Kyle was using both hands to play the piano, an instrument he'd never touched before except for some random pounding when he was really mad and Mom wasn't home.

Mom blinked at us, looked, listened, blinked again. She pointed to a corner of my picture where I had put a twisty ladder, one of the things the octoblob had shown me. "What's that, Iris?" she asked.

"I don't know. Just a picture."

Mom went to the bookshelf and got down

one of her med-school textbooks and opened it to a picture that showed a twisty ladder in four colors. "DNA," she said. "What makes everybody different, what makes life sort itself out."

It sounded like what the octoblob had told us, listening/looking at all the living things on Earth, finding out how they were different from one another.

"How did you know to make it like that?" she asked me.

"I guess I must have seen a picture somewhere." I thought of glimmering dots of light.

Kyle played a part of his song that only had four notes, but the way they sounded kept changing: his version of my ladder.

Mom didn't get it, though.

"Can I keep this book to look at?" I asked her, wondering if there would be any other pictures I could recognize.

"Sure, honey," she said. "I'm going to fix pizza now. Would you like to stay, Kyle?"

"Sure, Norma. Gotta call Mom, though."

While he went to phone, I started another picture, yellow dots on blue paper, of two star-people touching hands. I wondered how Kyle would play that on the piano. A surge of happiness washed through me that I had someone to share the experience with. I hoped the octoblob had gone to find its buddy.

Some stories stay with you, even if you've never read them. I can remember vividly a day in seventh grade when I went to school and heard the kids discussing an episode of The Twilight Zone *they had seen the night before. Thirty years later, while searching for material for this book, I was leafing through a collection of stories and spotted the tale that follows. I knew instantly that it was the story the kids had been talking about that day. I bought the book, took it home, read the story, and knew I wanted to use it here. I guarantee that once you read it, you won't forget it!*

TO SERVE MAN

Damon Knight

The Kanamit were not very pretty, it's true. They looked something like pigs and something like people, and that is not an attractive combination. Seeing them for the first time shocked you; that was their handicap. When a thing with the countenance of a fiend comes from the stars and offers a gift, you are disinclined to accept.

I don't know what we expected interstellar visitors to look like—those who thought about it at all, that is. Angels, perhaps, or something too alien to be really awful. Maybe that's why we were all so horrified and repelled when they landed in their great ships and we saw what they really were like.

The Kanamit were short and very hairy—thick, bristly, brown-gray hair all over their abominably plump bodies. Their noses were snoutlike and their eyes small, and they had thick hands of three fingers each. They wore green leather harness and green shorts, but I think the shorts were a concession to our notions of public decency. The garments were quite modishly cut, with slash pockets and half-belts in the back. The Kanamit had a sense of humor, anyhow.

There were three of them at this session of the U.N., and, lord, I can't tell you how queer it looked to see them there in the middle of a solemn plenary session—three fat piglike creatures in green harness and shorts, sitting at the long table below the podium, surrounded by the packed arcs of delegates from every nation. They sat correctly upright, politely watching each speaker. Their flat ears drooped over the earphones. Later on, I believe, they learned every human language, but at this time they knew only French and English.

They seemed perfectly at ease—and that, along with their humor, was a thing that tended to make me like them. I was in the minority; I didn't think they were trying to put anything over.

The delegate from Argentina got up and said that his government was interested in the demonstration of a new cheap power source, which the Kanamit had made at the previous session, but that the Argentine government could not commit itself as to its future policy without a much more thorough examination.

It was what all the delegates were saying, but I had to pay particular attention to Señor Valdes, because he tended to sputter and his diction was bad. I got through the translation all right, with only one or two momentary hesitations, and then switched to the Polish-English line to hear how Grigori was doing with Janciewicz. Janciewicz was the cross Grigori had to bear, just as Valdes was mine.

Janciewicz repeated the previous remarks with a few ideological variations, and then the secretary-general recognized the delegate from France, who introduced Dr. Denis Lévêque, the criminologist, and a great deal of complicated equipment was wheeled in.

Dr. Lévêque remarked that the question in many people's minds had been aptly expressed by the delegate from the U.S.S.R. at the preceding session, when he demanded, "What is the motive of the Kanamit? What is their purpose in offering us these unprecedented gifts, while asking nothing in return?"

The doctor then said, "At the request of several delegates and with the full consent of our guests, the Kanamit, my associates and I have made a series of tests upon the Kanamit with the equipment which you see before you. These tests will now be repeated."

A murmur ran through the chamber. There was a fusillade of flashbulbs, and one of the TV cameras moved up to focus on the instrument board of the doctor's equipment. At the same time, the huge television screen behind the podium lighted up, and we saw the blank faces of two dials, each with its pointer resting at zero, and a strip of paper tape with a stylus point resting against it.

The doctor's assistants were fastening wires to the temples of one of the Kanamit, wrapping a canvas-covered rubber tube around his forearm, and taping something to the palm of his right hand.

In the screen, we saw the paper tape begin to move while the stylus traced a slow zigzag pattern along it. One of the needles began to jump rhythmically; the other flipped halfway over and stayed there, wavering slightly.

"These are the standard instruments for

testing the truth of a statement," said Dr. Lévêque. "Our first object, since the physiology of the Kanamit is unknown to us, was to determine whether or not they react to these tests as human beings do. We will now repeat one of the many experiments which were made in the endeavor to discover this."

He pointed to the first dial. "This instrument registers the subject's heartbeat. This shows the electrical conductivity of the skin in the palm of his hand, a measure of perspiration, which increases under stress. And this"—pointing to the tape-and-stylus device—"shows the pattern and intensity of the electrical waves emanating from his brain. It has been shown, with human subjects, that all these readings vary markedly depending upon whether the subject is speaking the truth."

He picked up two large pieces of cardboard, one red and one black. The red one was a square about three feet on a side; the black was a rectangle three and a half feet long. He addressed himself to the Kanama.

"Which of these is longer than the other?"

"The red," said the Kanama.

Both needles leaped wildly, and so did the line on the unrolling tape.

"I shall repeat the question," said the doctor. "Which of these is longer than the other?"

"The black," said the creature.

This time the instruments continued in their normal rhythm.

"How did you come to this planet?" asked the doctor.

"Walked," replied the Kanama.

Again the instruments responded, and there was a subdued ripple of laughter in the chamber.

"Once more," said the doctor. "How did you come to this planet?"

"In a spaceship," said the Kanama, and the instruments did not jump.

The doctor again faced the delegates. "Many such experiments were made," he said, "and my colleagues and myself are satisfied that the mechanisms are effective. Now"—he turned to the Kanama—"I shall ask our distinguished guest to reply to the question put at the last session by the delegate of the U.S.S.R.—namely, what is the motive of the Kanamit people in offering these great gifts to the people of Earth?"

The Kanama rose. Speaking this time in English, he said, "On my planet there is a saying, 'There are more riddles in a stone than in a philosopher's head.' The motives of intelligent beings, though they may at times appear obscure, are simple things compared to the complex workings of the natural universe. Therefore I hope that the people of Earth will understand, and believe, when I tell you that our mission upon your planet is simply this—to bring to you the peace and plenty which we ourselves enjoy, and which we have in the past brought to other races throughout the galaxy. When your world has no more hunger, no more war, no more needless suffering, that will be our reward."

And the needles had not jumped once.

The delegate from the Ukraine jumped to his feet, asking to be recognized, but the time was up and the secretary-general closed the session.

I met Grigori as we were leaving the chamber. His face was red with excitement. "Who promoted that circus?" he demanded.

"The tests looked genuine to me," I told him.

"A circus!" he said vehemently. "A second-rate farce! If they were genuine, Peter, why was debate stifled?"

"There'll be time for debate tomorrow, surely."

"Tomorrow the doctor and his instruments will be back in Paris. Plenty of things can happen before tomorrow. In the name of sanity, man, how can anybody trust a thing that looks as if it ate the baby?"

I was a little annoyed. I said, "Are you sure

you're not more worried about their politics than their appearance?"

He said, "Bah," and went away.

The next day reports began to come in from government laboratories all over the world where the Kanamit's power source was being tested. They were wildly enthusiastic. I don't understand such things myself, but it seemed that those little metal boxes would give more electrical power than an atomic pile, for next to nothing and nearly forever. And it was said that they were so cheap to manufacture that everybody in the world could have one of his own. In the early afternoon there were reports that seventeen countries had already begun to set up factories to turn them out.

The next day the Kanamit turned up with plans and specimens of a gadget that would increase the fertility of any arable land by 60 to 100 percent. It speeded the formation of nitrates in the soil, or something. There was nothing in the newscasts any more but stories about the Kanamit. The day after that, they dropped their bombshell.

"You now have potentially unlimited power and increased food supply," said one of them. He pointed with his three-fingered hand to an instrument that stood on the table before him. It was a box on a tripod, with a parabolic reflector on the front of it. "We offer you today a third gift which is at least as important as the first two."

He beckoned to the TV men to roll their cameras into closeup position. Then he picked up a large sheet of cardboard covered with drawings and English lettering. We saw it on the large screen above the podium; it was all clearly legible.

"We are informed that this broadcast is being relayed throughout your world," said the Kanama. "I wish that everyone who has equipment for taking photographs from television screens would use it now."

The secretary-general leaned forward and asked a question sharply, but the Kanama ignored him.

"This device," he said, "generates a field in which no explosive, of whatever nature, can detonate."

There was an uncomprehending silence.

The Kanama said, "It cannot now be suppressed. If one nation has it, all must have it." When nobody seemed to understand, he explained bluntly, "There will be no more war."

That was the biggest news of the millennium, and it was perfectly true. It turned out that the explosions the Kanama was talking about included gasoline and diesel explosions.

They had simply made it impossible for anybody to mount or equip a modern army.

We could have gone back to bows and arrows, of course, but that wouldn't have satisfied the military. Besides, there wouldn't be any reason to make war. Every nation would soon have everything.

Nobody ever gave another thought to those lie-detector experiments, or asked the Kanamit what their politics were. Grigori was put out; he had nothing to prove his suspicions.

I quit my job with the U.N. a few months later, because I foresaw that it was going to die under me anyhow. U.N. business was booming at the time, but after a year or so there was going to be nothing for it to do. Every nation on Earth was well on the way to being completely self-supporting; they weren't going to need much arbitration.

I accepted a position as translator with the Kanamit Embassy, and it was there that I ran into Grigori again. I was glad to see him, but I couldn't imagine what he was doing there.

"I thought you were on the opposition," I said. "Don't tell me you're convinced the Kanamit are all right."

He looked rather shamefaced. "They're not what they look, anyhow," he said.

It was as much of a concession as he could decently make, and I invited him down to the embassy lounge for a drink. It was an intimate kind of place, and he grew confidential over the second daiquiri.

"They fascinate me," he said. "I hate them instinctively still—that hasn't changed—but I can evaluate it. You were right, obviously; they mean us nothing but good. But do you know"—he leaned across the table—"the question of the Soviet delegate was never answered."

I am afraid I snorted.

"No, really," he said. "They told us what they wanted to do—'to bring you the peace and plenty which we ourselves enjoy.' But they didn't say *why*."

"Why do missionaries—"

"Missionaries be damned!" he said angrily. "Missionaries have a religious motive. If these creatures have a religion, they haven't once mentioned it. What's more, they didn't send a missionary group; they sent a diplomatic delegation—a group representing the will and policy of their whole people. Now just what have the Kanamit, as a people or a nation, got to gain from our welfare?"

I said, "Cultural—"

"Cultural cabbage soup! No, it's something less obvious than that, something obscure that belongs to their psychology and not to ours. But trust me, Peter, there is no such thing as a completely disinterested altruism. In one way or another, they have something to gain."

"And that's why you're here," I said. "To try to find out what it is."

"Correct. I wanted to get on one of the ten-year exchange groups to their home planet, but I couldn't; the quota was filled a week after they made the announcement. This is the next best thing. I'm studying their language, and you know that language reflects the basic assumptions of the people who use it. I've got a fair command of the spoken lingo already. It's not hard, really, and there are hints in it. Some of the idioms are quite similar to English. I'm sure I'll get the answer eventually."

"More power," I said, and we went back to work.

I saw Grigori frequently from then on, and he kept me posted about his progress. He was highly excited about a month after that first meeting; said he'd got hold of a book of the Kanamit's and was trying to puzzle it out. They wrote in ideographs, worse than Chinese, but he was determined to fathom it if it took him years. He wanted my help.

Well, I was interested in spite of myself, for I knew it would be a long job. We spent some evenings together, working with material from Kanamit bulletin boards and so forth, and with the extremely limited English-Kanamit dictionary they issued to the staff. My conscience bothered me about the stolen book, but gradually I became absorbed by the problem. Languages are my field, after all. I couldn't help being fascinated.

We got the title worked out in a few weeks. It was *How to Serve Man*, evidently a handbook they were giving out to new Kanamit members of the embassy staff. They had new ones in, all the time now, a shipload about once a month; they were opening all kinds of research laboratories, clinics, and so on. If there was anybody on Earth besides Grigori who still distrusted those people, he must have been somewhere in the middle of Tibet.

It was astonishing to see the changes that had been wrought in less than a year. There were no more standing armies, no more shortages, no unemployment. When you picked up a newspaper you didn't see H-BOMB or SATELLITE leaping out at you; the news was always good. It was a hard thing to get used to. The Kanamit were working on human biochemistry, and it was known around the embassy that they were nearly ready to announce methods of making our race taller and stronger and healthier—practically a race of supermen—and they had a potential cure for heart disease and cancer.

I didn't see Grigori for a fortnight after we finished working out the title of the book; I was on a long-overdue vacation in Canada. When I got back, I was shocked by the change in his appearance.

"What on earth is wrong, Grigori?" I asked. "You look like the very devil."

"Come on down to the lounge."

I went with him, and he gulped a stiff scotch as if he needed it.

"Come on, man, what's the matter?" I urged.

"The Kanamit have put me on the passenger list for the next exchange ship," he said. "You, too, otherwise I wouldn't be talking to you."

"Well," I said, "but—"

"They're not altruists."

I tried to reason with him. I pointed out they'd made Earth a paradise compared to what it was before. He only shook his head.

Then I said, "Well, what about those lie-detector tests?"

"A farce," he replied, without heat. "I said so at the time, you fool. They told the truth, though, as far as it went."

"And the book?" I demanded, annoyed. "What about that—*How to Serve Man?* That wasn't put there for you to read. They *mean* it. How do you explain that?"

"I've read the first paragraph of that book," he said. "Why do you suppose I haven't slept for a week?"

I said, "Well?" and he smiled a curious, twisted smile.

"It's a cookbook," he said.

Little kids can get into the darnedest kinds of trouble, as Craig is about to find out. . . .

HOW I MAYBE SAVED
THE WORLD LAST TUESDAY
BEFORE BREAKFAST

Lawrence Watt-Evans

When I woke up last Tuesday morning and found out that it was only six-fifteen and my kid sister Karen was tugging at my sleeve, I was really mad. She wasn't supposed to be in my room *ever*, and especially not when I was trying to sleep.

"What do *you* want?" I growled.

"Craig, you gotta come downstairs *right now*," she said, not loud, but talking right into my ear.

"No, I don't," I told her, and I pulled the blankets up over my head.

"Yes, you *do*," she said. "You've gotta come and see what I found. You've gotta help me talk Mom and Dad into letting me keep it."

I blinked under the covers.

Keep it? Keep *what*?

I decided that maybe I'd better get up after all. Karen's five, just half my age, but she gets into twice as much trouble. This sounded as if it might be even more trouble than usual.

"Go away and let me get dressed," I said.

When I heard the door close, I got out of bed and threw on my jeans and a T-shirt as fast as I could. Then I went downstairs, and there was Karen, waiting in the front hall.

"Come on," she said, opening the front door.

"*Karen*," I said, "you aren't supposed to go out before Mom and Dad get up!"

"Just to the porch!" she said.

Well, that was probably okay, and anyway, she was outside before I could argue any more, so I followed her.

"Karen, what is this all ..." Then I stopped and stared.

She had it under the old laundry basket Mom had given her to keep toys in, and I couldn't see it very well, but I could see that it was moving, and that it was purple. Not a dull purple like maybe a lizard would be, but a really *bright* purple. I knelt on the porch and took a look through the plastic mesh.

It was furry and purple all over. It had six legs, and big yellow-green eyes, and some wiggly things that weren't exactly tentacles, but that was the closest thing I could think of. It was looking back at me.

It sounds scary, but it wasn't. It was really cute.

I wasn't really all the way awake yet, so I wasn't thinking very clearly, but I still knew there just *isn't* anything with six legs and purple fur, either cute *or* scary. My eyes got big as I stared at it, trying to figure it out, and it stared back.

"I'm gonna keep it," Karen said. "I'm gonna name it Roger."

"Karen, you *can't* keep it," I said. "We don't know what it *is*."

"It's *mine*," Karen said.

"Where'd you find it?"

"Here on the porch," she said, but she said it with the "you better believe this" tone that means she's telling a whopper. I decided not to argue about that.

"Well, you can't keep it. We don't know what it is, or where it came from, or anything. Maybe somebody's looking for it."

She got a stubborn look on her face. "Nobody's looking for Roger," she said. "If anyone around here had a pet like that, we'd have heard about it. Remember when Mr. Bester had that snake, and all the neighbors tried to make him get rid of it?"

"It's not the same thing," I said, but she was sort of right. I couldn't imagine how anyone could have had a thing like that without everyone in the neighborhood knowing about it.

In fact, I didn't think anyone could have a thing like that without everyone in the *world* knowing about it. *Purple* fur? *Six* legs?

I looked at the thing again, and it made a squeaky little noise.

I knew we couldn't keep it, whatever it was—Mom wouldn't even let us have a cat. I wasn't sure what to do about it, though. If we just turned it loose, it might get hurt. We didn't know where it came from, or anything.

But then I got to thinking about where it *could* have come from, and I could feel my eyes get even bigger. Even though it was the middle of July and the morning was already sunny and warm, I suddenly felt kind of cold.

"Karen," I said, "where'd you *really* find it?"

She just looked at me stubbornly.

"C'mon, you've gotta tell me!"

"Why?" she demanded, sticking out her chin.

"Because I think it must have come from outer space," I explained.

Then *her* eyes got big.

"Maybe they're going to invade us!" I said.

"What's 'invade'?"

"Try to take over and make everybody slaves. Like a war, kind of, only worse."

She looked at me as if I'd just said something really stupid. "*Roger* wouldn't hurt anybody," she said, pointing at the laundry basket.

I looked at Roger, and he blinked at me and made a sort of "Eep!" noise.

I had to admit he wasn't exactly a scary monster from outer space; he wasn't any bigger than Ms. Watson's cat Sugarplum, and I didn't see any fangs or claws or anything. And those tentacle things didn't look dangerous.

But if he wasn't a monster from outer space, what the heck *was* he?

"Well, maybe Roger's one of their slaves that got away," I said. "Maybe he's trying to warn us."

"He doesn't talk."

"He doesn't talk *English*," I corrected her. "Come on, we've gotta let him out of there."

"No!" she said. "If you let him out, Craig, I'll never speak to you again, and I'll go into your room and wreck all your stuff!"

"But, Karen," I said, "he's a monster from outer space!"

"He is *not*!"

"You don't know what he is!"

"Neither do you!"

Well, that was true. I couldn't think of

much of anything he could be *except* a monster from outer space, but maybe he was some kind of mutant or something, instead.

"C'mon, Karen, where'd you really find him? If you don't tell me, I *will* let him go." I grabbed the laundry basket as if I was going to lift it and let Roger out.

"Don't you dare!" she said, and she fell forward on top of the basket, holding it down. I was afraid for a second she was going to squash it, and Roger with it, but she doesn't weigh much, and the basket held up.

"Then tell me where you found him!" If I had to, I could pick up her *and* the basket, and she knew it.

"Promise you won't tell?"

I hate making promises like that, but I said, "Okay, I promise."

"Down by the lake."

I stared at her.

We live out at the edge of town, where the land starts getting hilly and woodsy, and if you go down to the end of the street and cut through Billy Wechsler's back yard, you can get into a state park, and right up to the edge of a big lake—Lake Cohoptick, it's called. We aren't allowed to go there without a grown-up along, ever since a kid almost drowned there when Karen was just a baby.

"You went down to the *lake?*" I said. I

tried to think of some way out of my promise not to tell Mom, because even though Karen's a real pain sometimes, I didn't want her to get herself killed. And besides, if Mom found out that Karen went there, and that I knew about it and didn't tell, *I'd* be in trouble. I'm the older one; I'm supposed to be responsible.

Karen must have figured out what I was thinking. "You promised!" she yelled.

"I know I did," I said. "Do you . . . I mean, is this the first time?"

She nodded. "There were these funny lights, and I wanted to see what they were."

"What were they?"

"I don't know. They were gone by the time I got there."

"But you found Roger there?"

She nodded again.

"Don't you see, silly? Those lights must have been the invaders' spaceship!"

She looked at Roger, and he squeaked again. "You think he was the invaders' pet, and he escaped and ran off?"

"Maybe," I said. I looked at Roger, and he looked back at me.

"You really think they were invaders?"

"Maybe," I said again. I didn't really know what to think. I frowned, thinking hard.

"Listen, Karen," I said. "Can you show me

where you found Roger? Maybe there's, you know, stuff to see there."

"We're not allowed down by the lake," she said doubtfully.

"You already went once," I pointed out.

It took me a few minutes to convince her, and I had to threaten to tell Mom and Dad about a lot of stuff, but at last she agreed. We put Roger in a box and took him along.

The hard part was sneaking through Billy Wechsler's yard, because Mrs. Wechsler was awake and getting breakfast. We saw her through the kitchen window.

Anyway, we got down near the lake, where there's a bunch of cattails and stuff, and some trees, and we were looking around when Karen tugged at my shirt and said, "Look!"

I looked where she was pointing, past some big bushes, and I started shivering and felt cold all over. I got bumps on my arms, the kind my dad calls gooseflesh, and I stood there frozen. I've never been so scared.

There were monsters walking along beside the lake.

Roger squeaked again, and I ducked down behind the cattails, holding the box shut. Karen crouched down beside me, and we watched the monsters.

There were two of them, with long bony legs and big glaring green eyes. They were purple, like Roger, only a little darker, but they were *big*, eight or nine feet tall, and they weren't cute at all. They were scary. They were stalking around on those great big legs like giant spiders, making hooting noises.

Karen started crying. "Those are the space invaders!"

"Hush!" I told her. I was afraid I'd start crying, too, if she didn't shut up. And I was even more scared that the monsters would hear.

"I bet they were gonna eat him!" she said.

"Well, shut up, or they still might!" I said. Roger would be just about the right size for a snack for those things, I thought, and I wished she hadn't suggested it.

She didn't say anything more, but she kept crying, only she was quiet about it.

I looked through the cattails and watched the monsters. They were walking back and forth, waving these long ropy things and hooting, and I supposed the hooting must be the way they talked, but it didn't sound like a language, not even like Chinese or anything, because it just seemed like the same sound over and over. They were looking down at the ground, and tramping along slowly and carefully.

I realized they were looking for Roger, and I figured they didn't want to leave any evidence around that would show they'd been there.

Roger would be pretty good evidence of *some-thing*, anyway. I thought about sneaking back up to the street and calling the police or somebody. I was pretty sure we could make it, but I didn't want to rush it. I didn't know how fast the monsters were. They were moving away, little by little, so the longer we waited, the safer we'd be.

Besides, I wanted to make sure I knew what they looked like so I could describe them.

They were purple and hairy; the bodies weren't actually much bigger than I am, but those six long long legs made them look huge. They had shiny white fangs, and these two ropy things.

And they kept hooting the exact same thing, over and over.

I frowned. I was thinking hard. I looked at the monsters, then down at the box.

"They look like Roger," I said.

"No, they don't," Karen said. "They're big and bony and horrible."

"But they've got the same number of legs and everything," I said. "And they're purple."

"So what?" she said.

"So I want to try something."

This was about the hardest thing I ever did in my life. I was still scared stiff, but I was pretty sure I had figured out something really important—what Roger was and why they

were looking for him. And if I was right, then I had to do it. It would be wrong not to.

And if I was wrong, we might all be dead, but my dad always says you have to do your best and then stick to your guns, not let anyone change your mind for you.

It was the hooting that convinced me. I stood up and called, "Over here!"

Karen screamed and started pulling on my arm.

The monsters turned around to look at me, and I thought they were about to run away—one of them even *started* running, a little, all those legs tangling together like some kind of complicated mixing machine. That was when I knew for sure that they weren't invaders from outer space; real invaders wouldn't have run. Real invaders would have zapped me somehow.

But then I held up the box, and Roger stuck his head out and squeaked.

The two monsters hooted in unison, that same hoot they'd been doing before, which I had decided must be Roger's real name. Then they *both* started running.

They were running *toward* us.

They hooted a lot as they ran, not just the same thing this time, but lots of different stuff. I don't know if they were talking to each other, or thanking me, or telling Roger how glad they were to see him, or telling him how much trouble he was in for running off, but they sure hooted a lot.

Karen was scrunched into a ball at my feet, screaming, but they didn't pay any attention to her; they ran up and snatched Roger out of the box and gave him the biggest hug I ever saw, using all four of those ropy things. Roger was squealing and squeaking like crazy. He looked really happy.

One of them untangled a ropy thing long enough to pat me on the head and hoot something very slowly at me. I said, "You're welcome."

Then the two monsters marched off, holding Roger between them.

Karen had finally quieted down, but she was still curled up on the ground with her hands over her eyes.

"Come on, silly," I told her. "You're missing it." I poked her with my toe.

She uncurled and sat up, and looked in time to see the water of the lake open up like a cellar door, and Roger and the monsters march down into the opening. Just before they were out of sight, one of them waved to me, and I waved back.

"They're gonna *eat* him!" Karen shrieked. She whacked me on the leg.

"No, they aren't," I said. "He's their *baby*, silly."

She got up slowly. "But he's so cute, and they're *ugly!*" she said.

I shrugged. "Babies are always cuter than grown-ups. Like kittens or puppies."

"But . . . aren't they invaders from outer space?" she asked.

I'd thought of that, when I was deciding whether to call to them. "Karen, do soldiers take their kids along when they're going to fight a war?"

Before she could answer, the ground started shaking, and we both fell down. A few minutes later there was this huge splash, and this gigantic big round *thing* came flying up out of the lake and went roaring off into the sky, lights flashing.

The lake water sprayed everywhere. We got soaked.

The spaceship, or whatever it was, took off, and we sat there dripping wet, watching it go, and Karen said, "Wow! It looks big enough to blow up the whole world!"

I nodded. It really did.

Now, probably it wouldn't have done anything anyway, because you wouldn't bring a baby along if you were going to go around blowing up planets, would you? But if they hadn't found Roger . . .

Well, maybe I saved the world last Tuesday.

But all I got out of it was grounded for a week, because Mom and Dad were up when we got home, and they were really mad when we came in dripping wet. And Karen's still sort of mad that I gave Roger back.

You know, one thing I still wonder about—after the spaceship took off, the lake looked half-empty. The water level was at least five or six feet lower. I mean, it was a *big* spaceship. So where'd all the water go when it first landed?

I guess I'll never know.

I don't care much, really; I'm just glad we're all okay and all together.

And so are Roger and his folks.

*This is a very weird little story, and every time
I read it I like it better.*

PIRATES

Mark A. Garland

It was Ronnie's turn.

"Pretend the spaceship is waiting for us on the launchpad, and it has Fast Drive so you can go to planets in just a few seconds!" he said. "And a mega-destruct bomb that can blow up a whole solar system!"

"But I wanted one of those big wooden sailing ships," Linda said with a pout.

"We did that before!" Ronnie said.

"And anyway," Timothy complained, "I always get stuck being the pirate when we do that. I'm sick of being the pirate."

"Pirates have all the fun," Linda said.

"Yeah," Timothy replied. "For a while. Then they get to lose the big sea battle."

"Anyway, it's my turn!" Ronnie said. "You promised I could have a turn!"

Linda sighed. "I don't know why."

"Because I haven't had a turn in—"

"You haven't had a turn," Tim interrupted, "because the last time we let you have a turn, you ruined everything. Like Linda said, you—"

"I said I was sorry!"

"Okay." Linda rolled her big dark eyes. "A spaceship. With Fast Drive!"

"And mega-destruct, and photon cannons, and—"

"Whatever," Timothy and Linda said at the same time.

Ronnie beamed.

The ship appeared. It was beautiful, long and pointy on the ends, fat and shiny in the middle, with rings suspended about it every fifty meters or so like Hula-Hoops frozen in time, and big fins along the back. The whole thing rested nose-up on a giant rail assembly that looked like a section of roller coaster.

They hurried aboard.

"Pretend we're webbed in and ready," Ronnie said.

Linda complained that her webbing was too tight.

"Are the controls set?" Ronnie asked.

"Set!" Timothy yelled.

"Blast off!"

The Fast Drive was just that. Stars swept

past, thousands of them. Linda waited as long as she could stand, then cried, "Where are we going, Ronnie?"

Ronnie shook his head as if he'd just found it. "Uh, pretend there's this planet, and we're coming up on it, zooming in. They can't detect us so we just land—"

Thrusters roared, hilly terrain swept up, then a gentle *thump* echoed through the deck.

"—and there's a princess who's supposed to rule the solar system," Ronnie continued. "But these space pirates have taken over her planet—"

"I'm *not* gonna be no space pirate!" Timothy shouted.

"No! No! Just *pretend* there are space pirates. And *we* have to rescue the princess."

"Good," Linda said, her mood vastly improved just now. "We'll pretend I'm the princess, and the pirates have me shackled with golden bracelets on gold chains that come out of the wall. And I'm just wearing this thing that looks like a bathing suit only with silver on it. The guards are these giant men with beards and axes and spears and laser rifles and huge muscles and—"

"Hold it!" Ronnie screamed. He and Timothy were staring pop-eyed at the view screen, the one that was tuned in to the secret monitor system that was always running at the evil palace where the princess was being held. "How are we supposed to rescue you from *those* guys?"

"You see? We just shouldn't ever let you have a turn," Linda said.

"No, we shouldn't let *you*!" Ronnie said, growing fierce.

"But it *is* your turn right now," said Timothy, pointing one finger at Ronnie. "So you just think of something. That's all. Go ahead. Something good!"

"Uhh . . ."

"Come on!" Linda snapped.

"Okay, pretend . . . pretend there's this very loud explosion outside. A pulse grenade. Tim throws it. And most of the guards run out to see. And there's a back door, so I can sneak in."

Then Linda was gone. The grenade went off, and Ronnie went through the back door to find Linda. Just as he reached her, someone shouted at him from behind. He turned and saw that it was one of the guards, an especially big, especially well-armored guard that Ronnie did not in particular recall.

"For touching the fabulous princess, you will die a thousand deaths!" the guard shouted. He pulled out his spear and his laser rifle.

Ronnie noticed a ridiculous grin on Linda's face.

"TIMOTHY!" Ronnie shouted.

Something flashed just where the giant guard stood—*had* stood—and Timothy stepped through the doorway. Smaller flashes arrived just to his right. "Laser rifles!" Ronnie yelped. He pretended he had a laser pistol of his own and blasted the locks off Linda's golden bonds. "Come on!" he snarled. "We're rescuing you!"

"Maybe," Linda said, not quite looking at him. "Maybe not."

Ronnie boiled. "My turn!" he squealed. "It's *my turn!* You always do this. Always, always!" Lasers flashed everywhere. Ronnie let out a lungful of exasperation, yanked at Linda's hand, and ran for the back door. Timothy ran behind him.

"They're at the ship!" Timothy hollered as the trio approached it.

"Jeeeze!" Ronnie howled.

"What a mess!" Timothy added.

"Okay," Ronnie said. "Pretend we got robots on the ship. And they come out and blast those guys!"

The robots were small and clackety, but they were excellent shots. Timothy walked backward, kept firing behind while Ronnie dragged Linda onboard. Then the door was closed, and the three of them were webbed in.

"Go, will you!" Timothy shrieked. "Blast off!"

"I *can't!*" Ronnie cried, pushing frantically at the controls, tears seeping out from the corners of his eyes. "I really, really can't! The controls are *frozen!*"

"I think maybe the guards fixed them," Linda said, snickering just audibly. "They are very resourceful."

The guards were all around the ship. The monitors picked up their voices. "Surrender!" they called. Ronnie looked at Linda, panic choking him, rage overwhelming him. *Again,* he thought, *she's doing it to me again!*

Linda scowled, shook her head. "You'll never get another turn ever," she said. "Never, never, ever!"

"I will!"

"Never, *ever!*"

"MEGA-DESTRUCT!" Ronnie screamed. . . .

It was Linda's turn.

Oh, great, she muttered. She let the words hang in the silence, then added, *Okay, pretend we exist.*

The legend of Elvis reaches beyond the stars . . . .

THE SECRET WEAPON OF LAST RESORT

Claudia Bishop

I'm lucky I didn't faint right there in the grocery store when I saw the headline:

ELVIS IS AN ALIEN!

How did they find out? I thought. For one gut-wrenching second I wondered if my little brother Davey had gone to the newspapers with the whole story. He *knew* I'd given up journalism forever because of the Elvis story. And he *swore* he would never tell.

Then I realized that the headline was in *The National Enquirer*, and stopped worrying. No one believes a paper that publishes stuff like "Goat Gives Birth to Human Baby." But then, no one else is the older sister of a kid like David Carmichael Ross. Davey. He's not just your basic red-haired, freckle-spattered eight-year-old in Spider-Man pajamas. On a good day he could give the monsters in the *Alien* movies a hard time.

On a bad day, he could level Chicago.

And of course, the fact that Davey has this awesome power to mess things up is only part of the problem. The other part of the problem is that the Elvis story is true. Sort of.

I grabbed the paper. This Elvis had been seen aboard a spaceship in Utah.

That's not the way it happened at all. . . .

The whole mess started when Mom and Dad's advertising agency invited my journalism class on a field trip to the Global Education Fair they were running.

"That would be a terrific place for the class to practice its reporting skills," Mr. Gonzales said happily. "Do you think your folks could arrange it for Thursday morning?"

"Thursday's the talent show," said Joey Schmidt, as if we'd all forgotten. Joey, Alex Frank, my best friend, Madeline, and I have a rap group called the Amazings. We'd been practicing all weekend for the show.

Mr. Gonzales raised his eyebrows. "The talent show is at two o'clock. The morning is still reserved for work, is it not?"

Yipes. There went any chance of the Amazings getting excused Thursday morning for a practice session.

Mom and Dad had to be at a meeting Thursday but they arranged the trip anyway, and the whole class ended up at the World Trade Center in downtown Manhattan that morning. The Global Education Fair was in the Center Atrium, which has soaring glass ceilings and lots of trees in big pots around the marble floors.

Things were looking great. Alex and I were going to team up to do our story. And the Amazings had *sounded* amazing when we'd practiced the night before. Only one problem loomed on the horizon. It turned out that Davey's school was having a day off for teacher meetings, and Mom had stuck him with Mr. Gonzales in return for her arranging the trip.

While we were waiting for the fair to open, I snagged Davey and said, "I hope you don't plan on tagging along with me all day, David Ross. I'm here to be a journalist, not a babysitter. You stick with Mr. Gonzales."

"So you can walk around and smooch with Alex Frank?" he sneered. Then he began to sing, "Noreen and Alex, sitting in a tree, K I S S . . ."

"Cut that out, Davey!"

" . . . I N G."

I glared at him. It was time for the Secret Weapon of Last Resort. The Secret Weapon works like this: You find out the one thing that most bothers a person about himself and get it out in the open for everyone to see.

For example, Davey has a superhero complex. When he looks in the mirror, he doesn't see an eight-year-old kid; he sees Spider-Man. I discovered the Weapon when a client of Mom and Dad's came to dinner and innocently said, "Oh, what a sweet little boy."

He was so offended he butted her in the stomach and got grounded for a week.

Davey was still rolling on with his song. "First comes love, then comes . . ."

I looked around. It was good that we were in a public place. The Weapon works best with lots of people around. Staring right at him, I said, "Be quiet . . . LITTLE BOY!"

Davey shut up. He glared at me. I could tell he was considering butting me in the stomach. Instead, he stuck out his hand and said, "Five bucks."

"Forget it, Davey. I'm not paying you just to stay away from Alex and me."

"Five bucks, or I'm Super Glue."

The little brat always wins these things. I groaned and dug into my wallet. "Two-fifty for now. The rest tonight."

The money disappeared into Davey's

grubby pocket, and he sort of melted into the trees.

Mr. Gonzales clapped his hands. "You have your assignments. Remember the questions for a good story: who, what, when, where, why, and how. The bus will leave exactly at noon, so be back here at eleven forty-five sharp. Okay, people? Let's get those stories!"

Alex came over and showed me a map of the fair. "We're supposed to cover the Student Foreign Exchange booth," he said. "You know, where students from other countries visit each other. The booth's in this far corner, here, behind a row of palm trees. Got the camcorder?"

"Right here," I said, patting the bag that hung from my shoulder.

"I'm going to get us a Coke," said Alex. "I'll meet you over there."

I started down the aisles, practicing with the camcorder. The exhibits all looked pretty much the same: three-sided cloth dividers with a table in the middle. I wanted more interesting stuff. When I rounded the palm trees and came to the Foreign Exchange booth, I found it.

The booth was great. The whole back wall was a movie of outer space. Galaxies shone like bronze flames against a rich blue night. Violet and green flashes of light streaked like comets across the sky. The entire booth hummed like a giant bee.

A sign hung over one of the stars:

STUDENT FOREIGN EXCHANGE
PRESS ENTER

It was the most fabulous thing I'd ever seen.

"Wow!" said a voice behind me.

I spun around. A totally obnoxious face peered at me from behind the palm trees.

"Beat it, Davey!"

"This is awesome," he replied, wriggling out of the palm trees and marching to the wall.

"Don't you touch that, David Ross!"

"But it's so *cool!*" said Davey, reaching up to pat the wall.

The bee-buzzing got loud. *Really* loud. A big hole opened beneath the entrance sign. Then a long, dark tunnel appeared, leading down into what looked like the depths of space.

I grabbed Davey and jerked him away.

Two cat-size points of light shone at the tunnel's end. They bobbed up and down, up and down, in a familiar kind of rhythm.

"They're walking up here," somebody said in a shaky voice. I realized the somebody was me.

"Toward us," whispered Davey.

The points of light grew to dog-size. I pulled Davey closer.

Suddenly I felt as if the air in my lungs was being sucked out by a giant vacuum cleaner. The tunnel flared with people-size light. Two spheres burst from the wall, whirled fiercely in the air, stopped, then vanished.

In their place stood two beings—an older one, who looked about my dad's age, and a younger one, about my age.

Odds seemed good that they were aliens.

The older one wore a silvery jumpsuit. He had short dark hair with a little gray in it. The younger one had greased-up black hair that fell partly over one eye. He wore a truly bizarre outfit: a white satin jacket with a jeweled collar and cuffs; tight white pants; and high-heeled boots. He carried a shiny white guitar, and when he saw us he lifted his upper lip in a kind of sneer.

"ELVIS!" yelled Davey.

He was right. This guy looked exactly like a very young Elvis Presley. The only thing was, his skin was kind of plastic-y. I don't know if this accounted for the stuck-up expression on his face. It was either that, or the guy was a real snot.

I cleared my throat, which seemed to have gotten stuck together, and said, "Welcome to Earth."

"Little boy," said the older one to Davey, "take me to whomever is in charge here."

Worried that Davey would butt even an alien in the stomach, I spoke up fast. "I'm sort of in charge here, sir. I'm Noreen Ross, reporter from the Manhattan Central Junior High newspaper."

The alien looked at me like I was a little green worm in a cup. "Little boy," he said to Davey, "who is this?"

Davey, whose lower lip was sticking out in a way that meant trouble for somebody, said, "My sister."

"She is a female?" said this alien, the way you'd say, "She is a glob of gum on my shoe?"

Davey blinked at that. "Well, yeah."

"Females do not address males unless given permission. Do you give her permission to speak?"

Davey's beady little eyes lit up. He grinned like a thousand-watt light bulb. "You mean you won't talk to her unless I say?"

"That is correct."

"Man," said Davey, rubbing his hands together. "Oh, man."

I dug into my wallet before he could even get the words *five bucks* out of his slobbery little mouth.

"A *girl* in charge," sneered the Elvis-alien.

I started to shout, "What planet are *you*

from, 'boy'?" when I remembered that Mrs. Coltrane, our social studies teacher, was forever saying we had to value cultural diversity. I figured that even went for bozos from space.

"I had grave doubts about this from the beginning, Beezar," murmured the older one. "Do you actually expect me to conduct business with a *female*?"

"You promised, Father," said the Elvis-alien in a desperate voice.

His father looked at him coldly. "I entered into an agreement with you, Beezar, and no one in our Family *ever* changes an agreement. You will receive school credit for participating in this exchange program. With luck, this may overcome your miserable grades so that you can graduate with the rest of the Family. But I doubt it."

I was embarrassed for Beezar. He was a snot, but even a snot didn't deserve this.

"I also doubt that this female can arrange a concert for your"—his father waved his hands in disgust—"what do you call it? Your *performance*."

I could hardly stand still. This story was fabulous! Remembering the journalist's questions, I said, "If you don't mind my asking, sir, who are you? Where are you from? And why are you here?"

"I am Nadir Zoraan," he said, as if I should

know this already. "This is my son, Beezar. Our Family is from the Arcturian sector, from a star system thirty light-years away from Earth.

"My son, Beezar, built a crude device to monitor Earth's television frequencies and became fascinated by your programs. Apparently this has inspired him to imitate one of your entertainers."

"What programs?" demanded Davey.

Beezar tossed his head, so that his greasy hair flipped over his eye again. "The best ones, man. *Gunsmoke. Leave It to Beaver. Mannix. Ed Sullivan.*"

"Those are *oldies*!" said Davey. "I wasn't even born when they put on those shows."

"Is that so?" said Mr. Zoraan. "Of course, the TV transmissions are thirty years old when they reach Beezar's receiver. Tell me, little boy—how old are you? Eighteen? Twenty?"

I thought Davey would bust a gasket with pride. "I'm eight!" he shouted.

"Far out!" said Beezar.

"How old are you?" I asked him.

"Like, forty-five, baby."

Clearly, their life-cycle was wildly different from ours. Looking eighteen wasn't such a big compliment to Davey when you saw it from the Arcturian view.

"Can you arrange a concert, young woman?"

asked Mr. Zoraan, clearly disturbed by the necessity of speaking to me.

"I'm not sure I understand."

"My son will receive course credit for his performance, which will be reviewed and rated on audience reaction. That rather primitive device"—he nodded at Dad's camcorder—"should provide sufficient record."

I had to work to keep from shouting. Here was practically the biggest story in the universe, and it was mine. In exchange for getting Beezar into the school talent show, I could demand an exclusive interview. I might be the first thirteen-year-old to win a Pulitzer!

Trying to act real casual, I said, "What about a concert at two o'clock this afternoon? I think I could arrange it, if Beezar will give me an interview afterward."

"Sounds cool," said Beezar.

Mr. Zoraan frowned at him. "Remember, you represent the Family. Do not disgrace yourself any more than you have already." He turned to me and snapped, "Young woman!"

"Yes, Mr. Zoraan."

"You agree to the Exchange?"

"Sure," I said, still thinking of my Pulitzer.

"Fine. The tunnel will remain open until four o'clock this afternoon. Return here by then." Then he snapped his fingers and said, "Little boy, come here!"

A sudden sickening smell filled the air. Yellow light flashed from the wall and swirled around us like a tornado. The whirling winds of light suddenly stopped. It was like being in the middle of a hollow cube of plastic. Mr. Zoraan raised his arm, which stretched and stretched into a long, flesh-colored snake. The snake-arm writhed around his shoulders as if he were winding up to throw a baseball. The arm snapped forward. The hand at the end clutched Davey's belt, jerked him into the air, and spun him around.

I tried to scream, but no sound came out.

"Hey!" yelled Davey.

I grabbed for him. His little jacket came off in my hands. I swung the camcorder at Mr. Zoraan. The bag hit the wall of light with a solid *thunck* as the snake-arm threw Davey into the tunnel.

"DAVVVVEYYYY!" I screamed, jumping after him.

I smacked into a solid wall of light.

My nose ached and my eyes watered as I stared into the tunnel. At the end I could see a little Davey-size ball of light bobbing up and down, up and down.

"GIVE ME BACK MY BROTHER!" I yelled.

"Cool it, sister," said Beezar.

"I'M NOT YOUR SISTER, YOU CREEP. WHERE'S DAVEY?"

"Miss Ross," said Mr. Zoraan icily, "stop that dreadful noise. No one can hear you, I assure you. May I remind you that you agreed to this Exchange?"

My heart sank. I had been so intent on getting the story I hadn't thought about what Mr. Zoraan meant when he asked if I agreed to the Exchange.

"NOT WITH MY BROTHER, I DIDN'T!" I cried.

The aliens just smirked at me. I stopped yelling. Screaming wasn't going to get Davey back. "Look, Mr. Zoraan, I made a mistake. The deal's off. I didn't realize that the Exchange meant Davey for your son. Please bring him back."

"Nonsense. Everything is perfectly in order. My schedule allows for one Exchange and one Exchange only. This is it." He glared at his son. "I told you this was a foolish idea. We will discuss it further when you return."

Then he disappeared into the tunnel.

The light barrier was gone. A red star shone in the wall where the tunnel opening had been. The sign now read:

EXCHANGE IN PROGRESS

That fat-head Beezar just stood and looked at me.

"If my brother is hurt I'll get you," I said. "I'll get you if it's the last thing I ever do. I'm going to call my folks, and then the police. I'm going to call the Army!"

"Then you will never see your brother again," said Beezar. "Do as I say, and you'll see him soon enough. Say, in ten years or so."

"WHAT!"

"I'm not going back to my father until I'm a star," said Beezar. He lifted his upper lip in a truly amazing sneer. "Nadir Zoraan thinks I am coming back this afternoon, but he is wrong, wrong, wrong. He doesn't believe in me. He laughs at me. But I am going to be a hit at this concert. Then I'm going to travel all over your planet and be a star. When I'm good and ready to go home, I will. Maybe in ten years, maybe longer, we'll complete the Exchange and get your brother back."

"You *jerk*!" I said fiercely. "I can't believe you'd do this to a little kid. He'll be scared to death!"

"Don't be silly. My mother loves babies. She'll take care of him." He stepped close to me, and an ugly green glow pulsed behind his plastic-y skin. "You are not to tell anyone about this, Noreen. If you do . . ."

He was interrupted by Alex Frank stepping

through the palm trees with two Cokes in his hands. "Hey, Noreen," he said. "Are you all right? You look kind of pale."

I gaped at him. He seemed so *normal.*

"Noreen?" he said again. Suddenly he took a good look at Beezar. "Uh . . . hi," he said, sounding puzzled.

Beezar curled his lip in his Elvis sneer. "What's howlin', Daddy-o?"

"This is Beezar, Alex. He's a . . . a foreign exchange student. I . . . uh, I thought he might make a good story for the newspaper, so I invited him to come back to school with us for a while."

"Where are you from, Beezar?" asked Alex, obviously remembering Mrs. Coltrane's words about respecting cultural diversity.

"Outer space, man," said Beezar, tossing his greasy hair.

Alex was quiet for a minute. "Right," he said at last. Then he turned to me and said, "Um, Noreen? Can I talk to you for a minute?"

We moved closer to the palm trees. I kept an eye on Beezar in case he did something weird.

"Noreen, you can't just bring this kid to school," said Alex. "What's going on here?"

I looked at Alex. How could I tell him the truth? But if I didn't get help, Davey would be trapped on some weird planet for the next ten years.

So I started to tell him what had happened.

"Beezar is *what*?" hissed Alex. And then, his voice rising, "Davey's *where*?"

"Noreen," said Beezar warningly.

"If you want to have that concert this afternoon, I'm going to need help arranging it!" I snapped.

We ended up telling Alex most of the story, leaving out the part about Beezar not planning on going back that afternoon.

"Okay, we'll have to smuggle Beezar onto the bus," said Alex finally. "All Mr. Gonzales will do is count heads, so if Beezar squashes down in back, we can just sort of substitute him for Davey. We'll have to tell the others something to get them to go along with it. And it will take some really fast talking to get him into the talent show. But we may be able to pull it off."

I managed to get Beezar onto the bus without Mr. Gonzales seeing him. The other kids thought adding a passenger was a hoot, and went along just for the fun of it.

As we drove back to school, I stared at Beezar. If thoughts could kill, he would have been writhing on the ground in excruciating pain. Instead he just sat squinched down in his seat, dripping dorky expressions like "Let's blow this pop stand" and "I'm gonna split."

Ideas for getting Davey back were racing through my head. Most of them were worthless. I kept coming back to one thing: the Secret Weapon of Last Resort. I felt terrible now about using it on Davey. If I got him back, I would never use it again. But I had no qualms about using it on Beezar. Only first I had to figure out what it would be for him.

Slowly a plan began to form. I am not the only person who thinks Alex Frank is totally cool. If I got Alex to act as if Beezar was the stupidest thing on this earth when he did his Elvis act, the other kids would follow along. A lot of them would just sit there and groan. A few, like Butchie Frielander and Marvin Croft, would get out the spitballs and the insults. They'd run him off the stage in total humiliation.

If I could get that on videotape, I'd have a pretty good Secret Weapon of Last Resort. And unless I got Davey back, I would show it to Beezar's father.

I almost felt sorry for Beezar. With a father like his, it's no wonder he wanted to go onstage and get applause from people he didn't even know. I might, too, if Mom and Dad treated me that way.

But sorry as I felt for this screwed-up

phony from outer space, I felt a lot worse about my baby brother. I mean, it's one thing to have to put up with his dorky behavior at home. It was something else altogether to have him lost on another planet.

At lunch Beezar jumped the food line, then snapped his fingers for me to pay. When I finally got the alien creep settled, I took Alex aside and told him the rest of the story, and my plan. Then I had to go off and convince Mrs. Coltrane to let Beezar into the show.

I found her zooming around backstage, clipboard in hand.

"Mrs. Coltrane?" I said. "Can I talk to you a minute?"

"This is a bad time, Noreen. Can't it wait?"

She really did look busy. Her hair was all frazzled.

"Beezar's doctor said it was really important," I apologized.

"Who?"

"His doctor. You know—his psychiatrist. He says if Beezar doesn't get to be in the show, he might blow."

"Blow?" asked Mrs. Coltrane, running her fingers through her hair.

"You know. Go all flooey. Nuts. Right in the gym. In the middle of the show, probably. He wants to do his Elvis act, and if he has to sit and just watch the other kids, it'll send him psycho for sure." I pulled at my lower lip. "He just came out of the hospital. He had this terrible accident. It's marked him for life, probably. You know how you're always saying we have to value diversity. We can't discriminate against Beezar just because he's loopy."

"Emotionally challenged," corrected Mrs. Coltrane. She glanced at her clipboard. "I wish the office would keep us posted when new students enroll," she muttered. "Well, I think I can squeeze him in. He's not going to act out onstage is he?"

"He's just terribly, terribly sad," I said.

She patted me on the shoulder. "That's all right, Noreen. If the doctor thinks this would be good therapy, we must do all we can to help."

So that was done.

By the time the talent show was supposed to start I was a nervous wreck. I was backstage with the Amazings, of course. Beezar stood in a corner, messing with his guitar and looking at us through half-shut eyes, as if to say, "You're gonna love this."

Madeline poked me and whispered, "Who is that geek?"

Before I could answer, the Amazings were announced, and we had to go onstage.

My heart was too worried about Davey for me really to do justice to our rap number. But we had practiced enough that I was able to get through it on autopilot. It must have worked, because the kids clapped a lot, and when we went offstage I felt a little better.

Then Mrs. Coltrane announced Beezar's Elvis act.

He walked onstage sort of bowlegged and slouchy. Then he said, in this phony Southern talk, "Ladies and gennumun, I got a li'l somethin' for yew . . . 'JAILHOUSE ROCK'!"

Then WHANG! He hit a couple of chords on the guitar, threw the hair out of his eyes, and sang about being in jail.

Alex and I started yelling "Off the stage, bozo!"

It didn't work. The kids loved Beezar's music!

My heart sank. The truth is, if I hadn't been so worried about Davey, *I* would have loved it. The beat was fabulous, and Beezar's voice was like thick soft cream with a howl in the middle.

I made a couple of nice juicy spitballs, and Alex (who has more practice with that kind of thing than I do) lobbed them onto the guitar.

No result. Beezar ignored them, and the kids were getting more excited by the moment.

Alex looked at me and shook his head.

Davey! I thought desperately, so scared I felt like I was going to throw up.

The kids started clapping in time to Beezar's singing—even Butchie Frielander.

Oh, please, God, I thought. *Please, please, please, I've got to get my little brother back!*

Beezar finished his song. The kids went berserk. Beezar threw his guitar in the air and caught it. Then he took about a million big sweeping bows.

"More!" screamed the kids. "More, more!"

So Beezar started in about how if we're lookin' for trouble, we've come to the right place, if we're lookin' for trouble, look right at his face. And then . . .

He took off his face!

That plastic-y-looking skin had been a mask. Now that I saw what was underneath, I decided Arcturians must be the grossest aliens in the universe. Beezar's face was all warts. His eyes were insect yellow. Spiderlike fringes came out of his nose. Worst of all were his teeth: They were mossy green. Globs of spit hung at the corners of his mouth.

A moment of silence hung over the auditorium. Then the real screaming started.

I got it all on tape: Beezar's face, the retching kids, the rapidly emptying auditorium. Mrs. Coltrane was the only one to stick around. She patted Beezar on the shoulder, and said how plastic surgery helped all kinds of accident victims these days, and she'd make sure the whole school wrote a letter of apology. Then she left.

Beezar smacked his lips and licked at the spit. "Thish ish reedikuloush!"

"Put your face back on," said Alex.

Beezar did. He glared at us. "I said, this is ridiculous! Do you have any idea how hideous Earthlings are to Arcturians? My father was right. You people are barbarians. Did I throw up and scream when I saw you and your revolting brother for the first time?"

"No," I said softly.

His face crumpled. "They didn't like the real me."

"They sure didn't," I agreed. "Maybe you'd be better off back home," I added.

He sighed. "Yeah."

I looked at my watch. "It's time."

I'm glad Alex's parents give him a lot of pocket money. Otherwise I don't know how we would have paid for the cab ride back to the World Trade Center.

Beezar didn't say much, but he looked nervously at the camcorder a couple of times. We got to the booth, and he pressed the sign over the red star. The tunnel opened. Spheres of light whirled around, then Davey and Mr. Zoraan appeared, safe and sound.

I just about cried. Davey looked smug. Mr. Zoraan looked pained and rubbed his stomach with a thoughtful look on his face. I bet he didn't call Davey "little boy" more than once in Arcturus.

"Well?" demanded Mr. Zoraan.

Beezar looked at me miserably. I stepped forward, fiddled with the Erase button on the camcorder, then ejected the tape. "It was a great concert, Mr. Zoraan. I didn't get the end, but I got the beginning and the middle. Here, Beezar. I'll bet you get an A."

Beezar smiled at me. "Thanks, Noreen."

I hugged Davey. "You okay?"

"Arcturus," said Davey blissfully, "was *cool!*"

The yellow light leapt out of the wall and whirled around us. Beezar waved goodbye. His dad took his hand, and they stepped into the tunnel.

"See you later, alligator," I said.

"After a while, crocodile!"

They vanished into the wall. A sign appeared over the red star:

EXCHANGE COMPLETED

Alex treated us to a cab ride home.

The next day I turned in the best story of my whole life to Mr. Gonzales. He told me I would be a pretty good writer if I worked at it. Not a reporter, he said, but a person who writes made-up stuff. So I got a C in journalism class. Mrs. Coltrane made the whole school write a letter of apology to Beezar's psychiatrist and gave it to me to mail, so I made up an address and "forgot" to put a stamp or return address on it.

Then I gave up journalism for a class in creative writing.

On top of everything else, my little creep of a brother never did give me back my seven dollars and fifty cents.

What's a tentacle or two among friends?

JUST LIKE YOU

Bruce Coville

Just because I've tentacles,
And my skin is ocean blue,
Don't think I don't have feelings
Just the same as you.

Every time I fall in love
My knees are filled with bliss;
And I pucker up my eyebrows
To give my girl a kiss.

The times we have a lover's spat,
My liver's always broken;
Many times I've cried my ears off
Because harsh words were spoken.

When I am suspicious,
My feet can smell a rat;
I try to eat nutritious,
Lots of sugar, salt, and fat.

Bruce Coville

My nose runs and my feet smell—
I've heard that yours do, too.
I shine my ears with gobs of wax,
Just the same as you.

When scared, I feel my skin crawl,
The way you humans do.
Mine comes back when I call it
(I hope that yours does, too).

Though you're rarely eight feet tall,
I don't look down on you;
I know we're really much the same—
Even though you are not blue.

Though he usually writes for adults, Ray Bradbury has always had a special ability to describe children and their interests— interests that are not always what adults would want, or expect. . . .

ZERO HOUR

Ray Bradbury

Oh, it was to be so jolly! What a game! Such excitement they hadn't known in years. The children catapulted this way and that across the green lawns, shouting at each other, holding hands, flying in circles, climbing trees, laughing. Overhead the rockets flew, and beetle cars whispered by on the streets, but the children played on. Such fun, such tremulous joy, such tumbling and hearty screaming.

Mink ran into the house, all dirt and sweat. For her seven years she was loud and strong and definite. Her mother, Mrs. Morris, hardly saw her as she yanked out drawers and rattled pans and tools into a large sack.

"Heavens, Mink, what's going on?"

"The most exciting game ever!" gasped Mink, pink-faced.

"Stop and get your breath," said the mother.

"No, I'm all right," gasped Mink. "Okay I take these things, Mom?"

"But don't dent them," said Mrs. Morris.

"Thank you, thank you!" cried Mink, and boom! she was gone, like a rocket.

Mrs. Morris surveyed the fleeing tot. "What's the name of the game?"

"Invasion!" said Mink. The door slammed.

In every yard on the street children brought out knives and forks and pokers and old stovepipes and can openers.

It was an interesting fact that this fury and bustle occurred only among the younger children. The older ones, those ten years and more, disdained the affair and marched scornfully off on hikes or played a more dignified version of hide-and-seek on their own.

Meanwhile, parents came and went in chromium beetles. Repairmen came to repair the vacuum elevators in houses, to fix fluttering television sets, or hammer upon stubborn food-delivery tubes. The adult civilization passed and repassed the busy youngsters, jealous of the fierce energy of the wild tots, toler-

antly amused at their flourishings, longing to join in themselves.

"This and this and *this*," said Mink, instructing the others with their assorted spoons and wrenches. "Do that, and bring *that* over here. No! *Here*, ninny! Right. Now get back while I fix this." Tongue in teeth, face wrinkled in thought. "Like that. See?"

"Yayyyy!" shouted the kids.

Twelve-year-old Joseph Connors ran up.

"Go away," said Mink straight at him.

"I wanna play," said Joseph.

"Can't!" said Mink.

"Why not?"

"You'd just make fun of us."

"Honest, I wouldn't."

"No. We know *you*. Go away or we'll kick you."

Another twelve-year-old boy whirred by on little motor skates. "Hey, Joe! Come on! Let them sissies play!"

Joseph showed reluctance and a certain wistfulness. "I *want* to play," he said.

"You're old," said Mink firmly.

"Not *that* old," said Joe sensibly.

"You'd only laugh and spoil the Invasion."

The boy on the motor skates made a rude lip noise. "Come on, Joe! Them and their fairies! Nuts!"

Joseph walked off slowly. He kept looking back, all down the block.

Mink was already busy again. She made a kind of apparatus with her gathered equipment. She had appointed another little girl with a pad and pencil to take down notes in painful slow scribbles. Their voices rose and fell in the warm sunlight.

All around them the city hummed. The streets were lined with good green and peaceful trees. Only the wind made a conflict across the city, across the country, across the continent. In a thousand other cities there were trees and children and avenues, businessmen in their quiet offices taping their voices, or watching televisors. Rockets hovered like darning needles in the blue sky. There was the universal, quiet conceit and easiness of men accustomed to peace, quite certain there would never be trouble again. Arm in arm, men all over earth were a united front. The perfect weapons were held in equal trust by all nations. A situation of incredibly beautiful balance had been brought about. There were no traitors among men, no unhappy ones, no disgruntled ones; therefore the world was based upon a stable ground. Sunlight illumined half the world and the trees drowsed in a tide of warm air.

Mink's mother, from her upstairs window, gazed down.

The children. She looked upon them and shook her head. Well, they'd eat well, sleep well, and be in school on Monday. Bless their vigorous little bodies. She listened.

Mink talked earnestly to someone near the rose bush—though there was no one there.

These odd children. And the little girl, what was her name? Anna? Anna took notes on a pad. First, Mink asked the rose bush a question, then called the answer to Anna.

"Triangle," said Mink.

"What's a tri," said Anna with difficulty, "angle?"

"Never mind," said Mink.

"How you spell it?" asked Anna.

"T-r-i—" spelled Mink slowly, then snapped, "Oh, spell it yourself!" She went on to other words. "Beam," she said.

"I haven't got tri," said Anna, "angle down yet!"

"Well, hurry, hurry!" cried Mink.

Mink's mother leaned out the upstairs window. "A-n-g-l-e," she spelled down at Anna.

"Oh, thanks, Mrs. Morris," said Anna.

"Certainly," said Mink's mother and withdrew, laughing, to dust the hall with an electro-duster magnet.

The voices wavered on the shimmery air. "Beam," said Anna. Fading.

"Four-nine-seven-A-and-B-and-X," said Mink,

far away, seriously. "And a fork and a string and a—hex-hex-agony—hexagonal!"

At lunch Mink gulped milk at one toss and was at the door. Her mother slapped the table.

"You sit right back down," commanded Mrs. Morris. "Hot soup in a minute." She poked a red button on the kitchen butler, and ten seconds later something landed with a bump in the rubber receiver. Mrs. Morris opened it, took out a can with a pair of aluminum holders, unsealed it with a flicker, and poured hot soup into a bowl.

During all this Mink fidgeted. "Hurry, Mom! This is a matter of life and death! Aw—"

"I was the same way at your age. Always life and death. I know."

Mink banged away at the soup.

"Slow down," said Mom.

"Can't," said Mink. "Drill's waiting for me."

"Who's Drill? What a peculiar name," said Mom.

"You don't know him," said Mink.

"A new boy in the neighborhood?" asked Mom.

"He's new all right," said Mink. She started on her second bowl.

"Which one is Drill?" asked Mom.

"He's around," said Mink evasively.

"You'll make fun. Everybody pokes fun. Gee, darn."

"Is Drill shy?"

"Yes. No. In a way. Gosh, Mom, I got to run if we want to have the Invasion!"

"Who's invading what?"

"Martians invading Earth. Well, not exactly Martians. They're—I don't know. From up." She pointed her spoon.

"And *inside,*" said Mom, touching Mink's feverish brow.

Mink rebelled. "You're laughing! You'll kill Drill and everybody."

"I didn't mean to," said Mom. "Drill's a Martian?"

"No. He's—well—maybe from Jupiter or Saturn or Venus. Anyway, he's had a hard time."

"I imagine." Mrs. Morris hid her mouth behind her hand.

"They couldn't figure a way to attack Earth."

"We're impregnable," said Mom in mock seriousness.

"That's the word Drill used! Impreg—That was the word, Mom."

"My, my, Drill's a brilliant little boy. Two-bit words."

"They couldn't figure a way to attack, Mom. Drill says—he says in order to make a good fight you got to have a new way of surprising people. That way you win. And he says also you got to have help from your enemy."

"A fifth column," said Mom.

"Yeah. That's what Drill said. And they couldn't figure a way to surprise Earth or get help."

"No wonder. We're pretty darn strong." Mom laughed, cleaning up. Mink sat there, staring at the table, seeing what she was talking about.

"Until, one day," whispered Mink melodramatically, "they thought of children!"

"Well!" said Mrs. Morris brightly.

"And they thought of how grown-ups are so busy they never look under rose bushes or on lawns!"

"Only for snails and fungus."

"And then there's something about dim-dims."

"Dim-dims?"

"Dimens-shuns."

"Dimensions?"

"Four of 'em! And there's something about kids under nine and imagination. It's really funny to hear Drill talk."

Mrs. Morris was tired. "Well, it must be funny. You're keeping Drill waiting now. It's getting late in the day and, if you want to have your Invasion before your supper bath, you'd better jump."

"Do I have to take a bath?" growled Mink.

"You do. Why is it children hate water? No matter what age you live in children hate water behind the ears!"

"Drill says I won't have to take baths," said Mink.

"Oh, he does, does he?"

"He told all the kids that. No more baths. And we can stay up till ten o'clock and go to two televisor shows on Saturday 'stead of one!"

"Well, Mr. Drill better mind his p's and q's. I'll call up his mother and—"

Mink went to the door. "We're having trouble with guys like Pete Britz and Dale Jerrick. They're growing up. They make fun. They're worse than parents. They just won't believe in Drill. They're so snooty, 'cause they're growing up. You'd think they'd know better. They were little only a coupla years ago. I hate them worst. We'll kill them *first*."

"Your father and I last?"

"Drill says you're dangerous. Know why? 'Cause you don't believe in Martians! They're going to let *us* run the world. Well, not just us, but the kids over in the next block, too. I might be queen." She opened the door.

"Mom?"

"Yes?"

"What's lodge-ick?"

"Logic? Why, dear, logic is knowing what things are true and not true."

"He *mentioned* that," said Mink. "And what's im-pres-sion-able?" It took her a minute to say it.

"Why, it means—" Her mother looked at the floor, laughing gently. "It means—to be a child, dear."

"Thanks for lunch!" Mink ran out, then stuck her head back in. "Mom, I'll be sure you won't be hurt much, really!"

"Well, thanks," said Mom.

Slam went the door.

At four o'clock the audiovisor buzzed. Mrs. Morris flipped the tab. "Hello, Helen!" she said in welcome.

"Hello, Mary. How are things in New York?"

"Fine. How are things in Scranton? You look tired."

"So do you. The children. Underfoot," said Helen.

Mrs. Morris sighed. "My Mink too. The super-Invasion."

Helen laughed. "Are your kids playing that game too?"

"Lord, yes. Tomorrow it'll be geometrical jacks and motorized hopscotch. Were we this bad when we were kids in '48?"

"Worse. Japs and Nazis. Don't know how my parents put up with me. Tomboy."

"Parents learn to shut their ears."

A silence.

"What's wrong, Mary?" asked Helen.

Mrs. Morris's eyes were half closed; her tongue slid slowly, thoughtfully, over her lower lip. "Eh?" She jerked. "Oh nothing. Just thought about *that*. Shutting ears and such. Never mind. Where were we?"

"My boy Tim's got a crush on some guy named—*Drill*, I think it was."

"Must be a new password. Mink likes him too."

"Didn't know it had got as far as New York. Word of mouth, I imagine. Looks like a scrap drive. I talked to Josephine and she said her kids—that's in Boston—are wild on this new game. It's sweeping the country."

At that moment Mink trotted into the kitchen to gulp a glass of water. Mrs. Morris turned. "How're things going?"

"Almost finished," said Mink.

"Swell," said Mrs. Morris. "What's *that*?"

"A yo-yo," said Mink. "Watch."

She flung the yo-yo down its string. Reaching the end it—

It vanished.

"See?" said Mink. "Ope!" Dibbling her

finger, she made the yo-yo reappear and zip up the string.

"Do that again," said her mother .

"Can't. Zero hour's five o'clock! 'By." Mink exited, zipping her yo-yo.

On the audiovisor, Helen laughed. "Tim brought one of those yo-yos in this morning, but when I got curious he said he wouldn't show it to me, and when I tried to work it, finally, it wouldn't work."

"You're not *impressionable*," said Mrs. Morris.

"What?"

"Never mind. Something I thought of. Can I help you, Helen?"

"I wanted to get that black-and-white cake recipe—"

The hour drowsed by. The day waned. The sun lowered in the peaceful blue sky. Shadows lengthened on the green lawns. The laughter and excitement continued. One little girl ran away, crying. Mrs. Morris came out the front door.

"Mink, was that Peggy Ann crying?"

Mink was bent over in the yard, near the rose bush. "Yeah. She's a scarebaby. We won't let her play, now. She's getting too old to play. I guess she grew up all of a sudden."

"Is that why she cried? Nonsense. Give me

a civil answer, young lady, or inside you come!"

Mink whirled in consternation, mixed with irritation. "I can't quit now. It's almost time. I'll be good. I'm sorry."

"Did you hit Peggy Ann?"

"No, honest. You ask her. It was something—well, she's just a scaredy pants."

The ring of children drew in around Mink where she scowled at her work with spoons and a kind of square-shaped arrangement of hammers and pipes. "There and there," murmured Mink.

"What's wrong?" said Mrs. Morris.

"Drill's stuck. Halfway. If we could only get him all the way through, it'd be easier. Then all the others could come through after him."

"Can I help?"

"No'm, thanks. I'll fix it."

"All right. I'll call you for your bath in half an hour. I'm tired of watching you."

She went in and sat in the electric relaxing chair, sipping a little beer from a half-empty glass. The chair massaged her back. Children, children. Children love and hate, side by side. Sometimes children loved you, hated you—all in half a second. Strange children, did they ever forget or forgive the whippings and the harsh, strict words of command? She wondered. How can you ever forget or forgive those over and above you, those tall and silly dictators!

Time passed. A curious, waiting silence came upon the street, deepening.

Five o'clock. A clock sang softly somewhere in the house in a quiet, musical voice: "Five o'clock—five o'clock. Time's a-wasting. Five o'clock," and purred away into silence.

Zero hour.

Mrs. Morris chuckled in her throat. Zero hour.

A beetle car hummed into the driveway. Mr. Morris. Mrs. Morris smiled. Mr. Morris got out of the beetle, locked it and called hello to Mink at her work. Mink ignored him. He laughed and stood for a moment watching the children. Then he walked up the front steps.

"Hello, darling."

"Hello, Henry."

She strained forward on the edge of the chair, listening. The children were silent. Too silent.

He emptied his pipe, refilled it. "Swell day. Makes you glad to be alive."

Buzz.

"What's that?" asked Henry.

"I don't know." She got up suddenly, her eyes widening. She was going to say something. She stopped it. Ridiculous. Her nerves jumped. "Those children haven't anything dangerous out there, have they?" she said.

"Nothing but pipes and hammers. Why?"

"Nothing electrical?"

"Heck, no," said Henry. "I looked."

She walked to the kitchen. The buzzing continued. "Just the same, you'd better go tell them to quit. It's after five. Tell them—" Her eyes widened and narrowed. "Tell them to put off their Invasion until tomorrow." She laughed, nervously.

The buzzing grew louder.

"What are they up to? I'd better go look, all right."

The explosion!

The house shook with dull sound. There were other explosions in other yards on other streets.

Involuntarily, Mrs. Morris screamed. "Up this way!" she cried senselessly, knowing no sense, no reason. Perhaps she saw something from the corners of her eyes; perhaps she smelled a new odor or heard a new noise. There was no time to argue with Henry to convince him. Let him think her insane. Yes, insane! Shrieking, she ran upstairs. He ran after her to see what she was up to. "In the attic!" she screamed. "That's where it is!" It was only a poor excuse to get him in the attic in time. Oh, God—in time!

Another explosion outside. The children screamed with delight, as if at a great fireworks display.

"It's not in the attic!" cried Henry. "It's outside!"

"No, no!" Wheezing, gasping, she fumbled at the attic door. "I'll show you. Hurry! I'll show you!"

They tumbled into the attic. She slammed the door, locked it, took the key, threw it into a far, cluttered corner.

She was babbling wild stuff now. It came out of her. All the subconscious suspicion and fear that had gathered secretly all afternoon and fermented like a wine in her. All the little revelations and knowledges and sense that had bothered her all day and which she had logically and carefully and sensibly rejected and censored. Now it exploded in her and shook her to bits.

"There, there," she said, sobbing against the door. "We're safe until tonight. Maybe we can sneak out. Maybe we can escape!"

Henry blew up too, but for another reason. "Are you crazy? Why'd you throw that key away? Blast it!"

"Yes, yes, I'm crazy, if it helps, but stay here with me!"

"I don't know how I can get out!"

"Quiet. They'll hear us. Oh, God, they'll find us soon enough—"

Below them, Mink's voice. The husband stopped. There was a great universal humming and sizzling, a screaming and giggling. Downstairs the audio-televisor buzzed and buzzed insistently, alarmingly, violently. *Is that Helen calling?* thought Mrs. Morris. *And is she calling about what I think she's calling about?*

Footsteps came into the house. Heavy footsteps.

"Who's coming in my house?" demanded Henry angrily. "Who's tramping around down there?"

Heavy feet. Twenty, thirty, forty, fifty of them. Fifty persons crowding into the house. The humming. The giggling of the children. "This way!" cried Mink, below.

"Who's downstairs?" roared Henry. "Who's there!"

"Hush. Oh, nonononononono!" said his wife, weakly, holding him. "Please, be quiet. They might go away."

"Mom?" called Mink. "Dad?" A pause. "Where are you?"

Heavy footsteps, heavy, heavy, *very heavy* footsteps, came up the stairs. Mink leading them.

"Mom?" A hesitation. "Dad?" A waiting, a silence.

Humming. Footsteps toward the attic. Mink's first.

They trembled together in silence in the attic, Mr. and Mrs. Morris. For some reason the electric humming, the queer cold light suddenly visible under the door crack, the strange odor, and the alien sound of eagerness in Mink's voice finally got through to Henry Morris too. He stood, shivering, in the dark silence, his wife beside him.

"Mom! Dad!"

Footsteps. A little humming sound. The attic lock melted. The door opened. Mink peered inside, tall blue shadows behind her.

"Peekaboo," said Mink.

*I think a good alien story should make you look
at the sky and wonder—which is exactly the way
this story affects me.*

CURING THE BOZOS

Sherwood Smith

"Here comes the nerd!"

"This ought to be *really cool* . . . not!"

The whispers were just loud enough for
every kid in the class to hear. I fumed, my ears
starting to burn as my little brother walked up
the row, his skinny shoulders hunched and his
glasses sliding down his nose.

The teacher beamed at him. "I've been
looking forward to your report, Frederic."

Of course she had. The teachers always
did, ever since they skipped him ahead into my
grade. But they never seemed to realize that
the more they talked about Fred's brains, the
more some of the other kids picked on him.

Fred gave the teacher a pained look, then
cleared his throat. "My research report," he
said, "is on UFOs."

"Yeah, because he's an alien!" Jason M. snickered.

"Class," the teacher said, frowning around. "Each one of us deserves the same consideration."

Ashley W. leaned over and whispered to me, "Lisa, did you know about this?"

I shook my head.

Watching Jason for approval, Ashley G. made snoring noises, and of course her best pals giggled obediently. Fred's shoulders hitched up another notch, and I was so mad my ears felt hotter than ever.

But Fred adjusted his glasses, then started. "My observations were made over a period of three weeks," he said. "I made three sightings, each on a Friday at about eleven P.M. The first one was an accident. I got up at eleven to get a drink of water, and when I looked out my window, I saw a roundish disk of light moving in the eastern part of the sky—"

"Yeah, just like a Frisbee," Jason whispered behind his hand.

Of course several boys laughed like maniacs.

"Class," the teacher said. "Continue, Fred, this is most interesting."

"So I've stayed up until eleven every night since. My second observation was made exactly one week later. This time I didn't turn on my bedroom light, and I had my camera ready. The UFO dropped through the clouds. It must have been about a hundred feet wide, maybe bigger, and it had green running lights—"

"Just like a blimp," Ashley muttered, and again came some laughs, though I could tell some of the kids were interested in spite of the loudmouths.

"I snapped a picture, but the flash attachment messed up, and before I could fix it, the UFO rose into the clouds and vanished," Fred said. "It's smeared because of the flash," he added apologetically, and held up a blown-up photo.

Not much of anything could be seen in it, which caused the class to laugh again.

"I think I see what might be your running lights in this corner," the teacher said kindly, touching the photo. Unfortunately, that part of the photo looked just like the street lamps around the corner from our apartment—and the class obviously thought so, too, because there were more snickers this time.

I bunched my long red hair over my ears, feeling as if they'd be steaming any minute.

"And my last sighting was a week ago," Fred said. "It was too foggy to get a photo, but I saw the outline of the ship, and the lights. It stayed in the sky exactly two minutes and fourteen seconds, then moved up and to the east."

"And you were mysteriously hypnotized so you couldn't call 911," Kyler sneered.

This time the class roared.

Fred dropped his report on his desk and shoved his glasses back up his nose. "Why would I call 911?" he retorted. "All they do is make noise with their sirens and loud-speakers—"

"And arrest you for prank calls," Demi F. said prissily.

"That will do, class," the teacher said. "Thank you, Frederic. That was quite interesting. Now, let's hear from Jason M."

Jason got up and bored on about basketball statistics, and most of the boys oohed and aahed like it was an inside report straight from a famous player.

Then it was time for recess. Fred followed the boys out.

Marissa and Kelly, my two best friends, were waiting at the door for me.

"Want to grab a volleyball court?" Kelly asked.

"Not just yet," I said. "I want to make sure Fred is okay."

Marissa squinted toward the field as we walked down the hall. "I don't see the boys," she said. "Anyway, I thought Fred's report was kind of cute. Did he make all that up?"

"Not Fred," I said. "Whatever he saw, he believes it was the real thing."

"Did you see it, too?" Marissa asked.

I shook my head. "None of us knew what he was working on. He told Uncle David and Aunt Pearl that it was a surprise, that he was conducting an investigation completely on his own."

Kelly nodded. "Pearl would like that—her nephew following in her footsteps with detective work. But why UFOs?"

"Uh-oh," Marissa breathed, and I swung around to look.

Jason and three of his buds, plus Ashley G. and two girls known for bullying kids, had backed Fred up against the fence. I headed straight over.

". . . teacher's pet," Jason was saying. "You didn't even do a real report—just made it up."

"I did not!" Fred yelled, his voice squeaking.

"You did, too, geek. Go on, admit it," Jason said, shoving Fred in the arm.

Since Jason is six inches taller than anyone in the class and a lot heavier as well, it didn't take much to make Fred stagger back. Jason's friends laughed nastily, and then Jason saw me.

"So, here comes big sister to protect the

little creep," he whined. "I suppose you saw Freddie frog-eyes' alien spaceship, Lisa?"

"If he says he saw 'em, he saw 'em," I said. "Now back off."

"Oooh, she's sooo-ooo tough," Jason said, hands on hips. "Gonna get some leather boots and a motorcycle?"

"Right after school," I said. "Want to help me pick them out?"

By then more kids had gathered, and several of them laughed.

Jason glared. "Look, everyone else had to do real work, and your teacher's pet baby brother gets away with fairy tales just because he skips grades."

"Fred does his work, and the teacher knows it," I said. "So just put your nose back in your own business."

Jason knew he was wrong, but of course he just had to push it, because half the class was watching. "Maybe it's time to see if you're as tough as you talk," Jason snarled, punching my arm.

Or he tried to, anyway. I sidestepped easily and put my hand on his wrist. Using his own muscle and force, I pulled him off balance so he fell sprawling in the dust, where he'd tried to make Fred fall minutes ago.

"So you like rough stuff?" he yelled.

"I hate it," I said. "But nobody pushes me

around. Or my family. Or my friends. Okay?"
I made my voice even on the last word and
held out a hand to pull him up.

He ignored it, scrambling to his feet and
glaring over his shoulder at me as he walked
away. The crowd of kids broke up.

"Come on, let's play some volleyball," I
said to Kelly and Marissa.

On the bus home after school, Fred was
quiet and gloomy.

When we settled into our bus seats, I said
over the usual howls and screeches, "You
okay?"

We both ducked some flying gym socks.

"I guess," he said. And then, quickly, "No
one believes me. Not even the teacher. I got a
B, and a comment 'Wonderful imagination.'
And I had field notes and everything." He
looked up at me, his brown eyes huge behind
his glasses. "Do you believe me, Lisa?"

"It might have been some kind of mistake," I said.

"A mistake?" He looked really upset. "You
think I faked it, too?"

"Oh, I believe you saw something," I said,
thinking fast. "But maybe it was some kind of
secret military test, or something. You gotta
remember that I wasn't there," I said. "Why
didn't you wake me up?"

"I really wanted to get proof, and on my

own," he said. "Like Aunt Pearl. I mean, no one else in the family seems to believe in life on other planets like I do, so when I saw the ship . . ."

"So what about your proof?" I asked.

"Well, the things I tried obviously didn't work, but the report was due today, so I did the best I could. But I'm not giving up," he said quickly. "Promise you won't laugh?"

"Promise," I said.

"I've set up a radio receiver, as wide a band as I can get," he said, grinning. "*And* the videocam. So far the visits have all been on Fridays, so they should come again tonight. Want to stay up with me and watch?"

"Sure," I said. "Sounds cool."

He blurted, "Thanks for sticking up for me today."

"No problem. I know you'd do the same for me."

"Except I never have," he said, his round face earnest. "It's always you protecting me, either here at school, or at the playground, or on the street." He stuck out a skinny arm, frowning at it. "I don't think I could protect a kitten," he finished morosely. "I wish you'd show me those tricks you learned in the Orphanage. Then I could smash that Jason a good one."

"Maybe someday," I said.

"They taught you cool stuff." He made a fist. "All I ever learned before my parents died was how to read when I was too young. I *feel* like an alien," he burst out.

I laughed. "I think we all do. I know I did when Pearl and David first adopted me and the kids at school made fun of my red hair."

"I don't think it's weird." Fred looked critically at me. "I think it's nice," he added with his shy smile. "In fact, I liked it when you came—and it was a *lot* redder then."

I grinned back at him. "Well, I could dye it green," I said, which made him grin. "You could, too, and I bet Pearl and David would love to do theirs as well. Then we could *really* be an alien family."

Fred laughed, his real laugh, and I knew he was all right again.

Then he surprised me. "What was it like? In the Orphanage."

When they first brought me home, Pearl and David told me about Fred. His mom (Aunt Pearl's sister) and his dad had been vulcanists. They'd been filming a volcano three years ago when it erupted and killed them. So Fred came to live with Pearl and David, and he was so unhappy they decided to adopt him a brother or sister close to his age. When they came to the Orphanage, we'd all liked each other right away.

"He almost never talks about his former life," Pearl had told me. *"We think it best if you let him bring it up when he's ready."*

"The Orphanage was okay," I said. "A lot of kids from very different backgrounds. It was pretty much like school around the clock. And all we seemed to talk about was what kind of family might pick us, and what we hoped for. I'm lucky—I got exactly what I wished for," I added.

I waited for him to talk about his real parents and his old life, but he just sighed and settled back in the seat. "We do have an alien family," he said happily.

"You mean you and me, because we're orphans?"

"And David draws cartoons all night, and Pearl chases bad guys." He sighed. "Or maybe Jason and those crumbums are the aliens. I don't know. I just don't fit in at school."

"Do you really want to fit in with them?" I asked. "I mean, wouldn't you rather they learn to be your kind of normal, than you dumb down and act like them?"

The bus lurched to a stop, and we grabbed our stuff and got out.

"*Sure* they'll learn to be decent—and pigs will fly out of my nose," Fred grumped, settling his books with one hand and his glasses with the other. "Well, forget them. I think I'll go to the library before dinner and see if that new book on astrophysics is in yet."

"Okay," I said, leading the way to the apartment. "I guess I'll just get started on my homework. And tonight, we'll listen for aliens."

Fred seemed pretty cheerful again as we went inside. David had a snack waiting, and as we ate, I wondered why Jason and the rest couldn't see in Fred what I did. I didn't know any other kid his age who was trying to teach himself calculus and reading every book on space physics that he could find.

"So how'd that mysterious report go?" David asked at dinner.

"Okay," Fred said. "My problem was, I didn't convince anyone." Then he grinned at Pearl. "I'm still tracking my proof, and when I have my info, I'll show it to you."

She grinned back. "That's what a good detective does," she said, looking pleased. Fred beamed.

He didn't say anything more, though, and at bedtime he just went into his room as usual.

Pearl went to sleep at nine-thirty, as she had to be up early the next morning. David shut himself into his study and put on his headphones, which meant he was out of this world.

Still, I waited until ten-thirty, then got out

of bed and went to Fred's room without turning on any lights.

The moonlight was clear and strong. Fred sat on his bed in his PJs, his glasses winking as he adjusted something that had faintly glowing dials.

"Hi," I whispered. "All ready?"

"I'm just testing my radio equipment," he said. "Want to see?"

I nodded, and he flicked on his little flashlight and shined it proudly over the wires and components. He'd put together parts from two or three electronics kits, and as he explained his setup to me, I thought about just how smart he was, and how determined he was to make his dream become real.

". . . so I figure they must use some kind of radio waves if they are sending communications at all," he was saying. "And they must be, don't you think? I mean, why else would one ship just appear like that, and hang around? They have to be communicating with someone."

"Makes sense to me," I said, sitting on the other end of his bed.

He had his window wide open, and cold air drifted in. Despite being so skinny, Fred didn't seem to notice, but I'm sensitive to chilly wind, and my feet and fingers and ears were cold. I pulled my hair close to my face to

keep my ears from hurting, and tucked my feet under me.

"There," Fred said, moving to the window. "And the videocam is ready, and I've got it set for night exposure. This time I won't mess up."

"What will you do if you get them on tape?" I asked.

"The first thing is, I'll show those scumbags at school," Fred said fiercely. "And then—I don't know. A TV show? Or maybe call the college and talk to the astrophysics department. Except who'll listen to a kid?" he finished bitterly. "Maybe I'll just try to communicate with them myself."

"That might be fun," I said. "What would you tell them?"

"What it's like to be a kid on Earth." He grinned, flicking his flashlight off. "I don't know anything else!"

"You're learning—about space," I reminded him.

"But they'd already know that stuff, or they wouldn't be here," he said, sounding impatient. Almost immediately he grinned again. "Sorry, Lisa. I'm trying to be logical about these things."

"It's okay," I said. "I think this is real exciting, and my mind keeps filling with questions."

He sat down on the bed, hugging his knees

close to his stomach. "Me, too," he said. "Like, what if I contact them, and they threaten to take over the Earth, and no one believes me?"

"That kind of alien would probably fire first and make demands later," I said soothingly. "And they'd take over a radio station or something, or beam the message off satellites. *And* they wouldn't try to take over a planet with just one ship. You didn't see a fleet, did you?"

"No, just one."

"But . . . what if they're nice, but their natural form is really disgusting?" I asked. "Like a bucket of snot?"

"Iccch," he said. "I don't know. I wouldn't shake hands, though."

We both laughed.

Then he said, "I guess I didn't tell anyone about the first one because I didn't really believe it myself. And then after the second time, I kept hoping they'd take me away." He got up again and circled around his room, touching wires and things.

"You wouldn't miss us?"

"Sure," he said quickly. "But they'd bring me back. At least, that's what I thought in my mind. You never know, of course. That's what's so exciting! Another world . . . different people . . . *anything* can happen. But I just

don't want their first contact to be with someone like Jason."

"Well, on a planet with like four billion
people, the chances are awfully good they'll get
a bozo for their first contact," I said.

"I know," Fred admitted. "That bothers
me, too. But there's no way to fix that, except
to try to be the first one."

"Well, either that, or try to help the world
cut down on its bozoness, and be more like
something space visitors wouldn't put in one
of their horror movies," I said.

Fred snorted. "Yeah, sure. I mean, it
sounds great, but there's no way one person
can make any difference at all."

"Gandhi didn't think so," I said. "Or the
Buddha, or Saint Francis. And then there's al-
ways the bad guys, like Hitler, or Genghis
Khan—"

"Okay, okay," Fred said with a laugh.
"Hey—it's nearly eleven. We'd better be
quiet."

He stopped at the window, looking out. In
the moonlight I could see his profile. He was
thinking hard.

I got up and joined him, my hands over
my ears in the frosty night air.

For a long time we watched the sky. Some
ghostly white clouds drifted by, but otherwise
the stars twinkled peacefully.

Fred whispered after a time, "How *would* you cure the bozos?"

"I don't know," I whispered back. "But it's worth working on, don't you think?"

Fred shrugged, his eyes ranging back and forth across the sky. Fifteen minutes passed . . . twenty . . . half an hour. Fred yawned once, then twice.

Finally he said out loud, "I guess it's no good. They're not coming."

"Maybe we ought to get some sleep," I said. "We can always try again, can't we?"

"You do believe me, don't you, Lisa?" He grabbed my arm, his fingers icy cold.

"You've never lied to me, Fred," I said. "I believe you."

He sighed, then turned to shut his window and climb into bed.

I went out, but instead of going to my room, I waited outside of his, listening. After just a few minutes his breathing changed into the deep, regular breathing of sleep.

So I went to my room and opened my own windows, looking up at the peaceful night sky.

I thought about what a tremendous task it would be, to change a big, confusing, frightening, exciting, wonderful world like Earth, to find some way to help human beings be ready to take their place among the worlds of the universe.

But that was my job. They'd picked us, orphans from all over the galaxy, and trained us on the ship we'd called the *Orphanage*, before they'd scattered us in various homes across many worlds. Our first goal was to find the potential leaders and encourage them.

I rubbed my ears, then pulled my hair away so my ears could extend in antennae form. As soon as my signal went out, my ship appeared, and I began sending them my weekly report.

You've been seen. We'll have to be more careful, but maybe it wasn't such a mistake after all. . . .

ABOUT THE AUTHORS

WILLIAM HOWARD SHETTERLY's novels include the young adult books *Elsewhere* and *Nevernever*, which are about runaways, elves, and magic that doesn't always work right. Born in Columbia, South Carolina, on August 22, 1955, he now lives in Minneapolis, Minnesota, with his beloved wife, Emma Bull (also a science fiction writer), and his tolerated cats, Chaos and Brain Damage. Anyone who saw his brief appearance in the film "Toxic Zombies" will understand why he decided to become a writer.

JACK C. HALDEMAN II lives on a farm in Florida with his wife, Vol, and an assortment of animals, both wild and domestic. He has written over a hundred short stories. His most recent adult novel is *High Steel*.

NINA KIRIKI HOFFMAN grew up in Southern California, but now lives and writes in Oregon. She is the sixth of seven children. She has sold almost a hundred stories and has written one young adult book, *Child of an Ancient City*, with Tad Williams.

DAMON KNIGHT's work as writer, editor, critic, and teacher has made him one of the most influential voices in the science fiction field for over four decades. Founder of the Science Fiction Writers of America, he is still a much-beloved rascal and gadfly for that organization.

LAWRENCE WATT-EVANS lives in Maryland with his wife, one son, one daughter, a cat named Willet Byte, a parakeet named Robin, and about 8,000 comic books, mostly horror comics from the 1950s and 1960s, many of which have stories about invaders from outer space. If you walk to the end of his street, cut through a back yard, and walk along a stream for about a quarter of a mile, you'll come to Lake Clopper, which (so far as he knows) does not have a spaceship under it.

MARK A. GARLAND read a copy of Arthur C. Clarke's *The Sands of Mars* when he was twelve and proceeded to exhaust the local library's supply of science fiction. Eventually he tried writing short stories of his own, but got sidetracked into working as a rock musician and a race car driver. Finally he came back to science fiction and has sold two novels and over two dozen short stories. Mark lives in Syracuse, New York, with his wife, their three children, and (of course) a cat.

CLAUDIA BISHOP is a young writer who lives on a horse farm in upstate New York. An herbologist and former dancer, she currently studies martial arts and weaving. This is her first story for young readers.

RAY BRADBURY lives in Los Angeles. He sold his first story over fifty years ago, when he was only twenty. Still actively writing, he is beloved throughout the world as one of the most poetic science fiction writers of all time. In addition to his short stories, he has written plays, novels, poetry, and the script for the 1956 film version of *Moby Dick.*

SHERWOOD SMITH lives in California. She began making books out of paper towels when she was five—usually stories about flying children. She started writing about another world when she was eight, and hasn't stopped since. She has stories in several anthologies, and has published two fantasy novels for young readers: *Wren to the Rescue* and *Wren's Quest.*

JOHN PIERARD, illustrator, lives with his dogs in a dark house at the northernmost tip of Manhattan. He has illustrated *Bruce Coville's Book of Monsters* and several books in the *My Teacher Is an Alien* series. His pictures can also be found in the popular *My Babysitter Is a Vampire* series, in the *Time Machine* books, and in *Isaac Asimov's Science Fiction* magazine.

BRUCE COVILLE was born and raised in a rural area of central New York, where he spent his youth dodging cows and chores, and dreaming about going to other planets. He now lives in an old brick house in Syracuse, with his wife, illustrator Katherine Coville, and enough children and pets to keep life interesting. Though he has been a teacher, a toymaker, and a gravedigger, he prefers writing. His dozens of books for young readers include the bestselling *My Teacher Is an Alien* quartet, as well as the *Camp Haunted Hills* books, *Goblins in the Castle*, *Jennifer Murdley's Toad*, *Aliens Ate My Homework*, and *Jeremy Thatcher, Dragon Hatcher*.